Border Crimes is based on the author's experiences, people he has known and historical events beginning with the years he lived in West Virginia attending college from 1958 to 1964.

To increase the reader's pleasure, we recommend first reading the Author's Notes in the back of the book that provide background information on each story without giving anything away.

Disclosure. The author was not involved in any of the crimes described in this book and never spent more than one night in jail.

Border Crimes

and Other Stories

Tales of Irony and Retribution

Bob Sherman

North Cove Press
North Smithfield, Rhode Island

Library of Congress Control Number 2017916077

Publisher's Cataloging-In-Publication Data
(Prepared by The Donohue Group, Inc.)

Names: Sherman, Bob, 1939-
Title: Border crimes and other stories: tales of irony and
retribution / Bob Sherman.
Description: North Smithfield, RI: North Cove Press, [2017]
Identifiers: ISBN 9780999543603
Subjects: LCSH: Crime--United States--History--Fiction. | Irony-
Fiction. | Retribution-Fiction. | LCGFT: Detective and mystery fiction. |
Short stories. | Humorous fiction.
Classification : LCC PS3619.H4642 B67 2017 | DDC 813/.6--dc23

10 9 8 7 6 5 4 3 2 1

Border Crimes is also available as an eBook at Amazon.com.

Photos and Cover Design by Bob Sherman

Dedication

This book is dedicated to my wife, Lisa Sherman, who provided consistent encouragement, and without whom, these stories would not have been completed or published. Thank you.

Table of Contents

West Virginia

Hanging Bridge *1947*   1

The Reporter *1955*   14

Restitution *1959*   31

The Last Foxhole *1961*   47

North Carolina

Self Improvement *2003*   59

New Hampshire

The Deer Stand *1978*   73

Rhode Island

The Boss's Wife *1979*   87

Perfect Crime *1985*   101

Greater Good 1982   115

Guilty Party *1986*   127

Border Crimes *1959*   145

Seventy-Five Cents
   on the Dollar *1982*   173

West Virginia 1947

Hanging Bridge

The first time I expected to outright die, we were dug into Salerno Beach with bullets flying overhead and kicking up sand on both sides. A German Mauser 7 mill knocked my helmet off and spun it out of reach, so I grabbed one close by without looking left or right for what I'd see.

The Third Rangers were sent to mop up the Germans and take back Rome. They told us it wouldn't take much, but we were met with machine gun fire and sniper rounds that took every third man the first day. My fear was so deep, I believed this to be the end, until I was close enough to see the enemy, which brought some relief knowing I was fighting men like myself and not something I couldn't see that could take my life without ever knowing who it was. It probably doesn't make sense now, but that's how I felt then.

Rome was liberated, and what was left of that city beckoned with food, wine and grateful citizens. Once settled, I got back to playing poker with men who thought they could beat a hick like me from West Virginia. I spent some winnings in town for favors and stayed on after the war, interpreting for displaced families while we helped rebuild where we could.

A year later, I returned home with enough money to buy a small house above the Monongahela River and a 46' Ford Coupe with a chrome grill and white-walls that took me back and forth between Charlestown and Wheeling in search of high-stakes games. There were plenty around to make a living. and I was only gone two weeks a month.

Sometimes I think about what else I might do, but not often. I survived the war, and that was enough for me. Winning streaks don't last forever. I keep my head down and don't ask a lot of questions, not because I don't care, but because I don't want to be involved in more than I was meant to be, or experience any more misery than I have, or cause anyone harm they don't deserve.

There are five houses on our road between the river and the railroad track. Families most often kept to themselves, taking care of their gardens and hunting deer. One or two earned a little money in town. My house is the first on the left after you cross the bridge. The trees along the side let you get down the bank to the water's edge without being seen, which some of the kids take advantage of now and then.

When I play poker in town, the sheriff doesn't bother me as long as there's no money on the table. He just likes to know where everybody is. He keeps track of those that need watching and lets his younger deputies keep track of single women to keep domestic disputes to a minimum.

I was looking at my empty glass, deciding whether to get another beer or some fresh air, but considering the sheriff was still inside and talking with his favorite waitress, I decided to stay put until he left. I figure the more he saw me staying out of trouble, the more points I rack up for the future. My buddy called it paying for living-insurance, which is no different than anywhere else.

Down in these parts, every town has at least one preacher, lawyer, car salesman, alcoholic and a gambler, an everyone's doing the best they can to survive. There were also men working the mines, and men who owned them.

One owner, Ike, was well known for keeping his mine open until it wasn't worth a nickel, then closing it down with a stick of dynamite. But his last one, he closed before the veins ran out, and no one knew why until they learned he partnered-up with Bobby Thompson who used the empty shaft to run a still. He made good moonshine and had steady customers while his silent partner, Ike, slept in late collecting his share of the profit.

The fact is people prefer the taste of alcohol that hasn't been taxed by a government that hasn't learned to mind its own business. The sheriff never bothered him, and the state police only showed up when someone bore a grudge. There is an order, natural or not, that is sometimes best left undisturbed.

Bobby traveled the same roads I did, but it was Wheeling that got him in trouble. Wheeling was controlled by a family that wanted him out of the city. So, when someone died of alcohol poisoning, and it was somebody's girlfriend, Bobby got the blame.

The second time I faced death, my hands were tied, and a gun was pointed at my head. This was about as certain as it gets.

It was an August night when a car stopped in the middle of the bridge, its lights shining through my bedroom window. I slipped through the side door and out behind a tree and watched three men walk down the road past my house to where Bobby lived.

A few minutes later they led Bobby to the bridge and his wife down to the river's edge. For a while, I only saw two men until one came up behind me carrying a gun. I couldn't tell you what I was feeling the most, fear or anger, but it was strong. We walked out on the bridge where I stood next to Bobby while they tied my hands.

One of the men opened the trunk and took up a rope. He tied one end to the railing and the other around Bobby's neck, then threw him over the edge where he was left to hang while his wife watched from below.

I resigned myself to death with the consolation, that a bullet was preferable to hanging. On the other hand, I was an innocent bystander who didn't deserve to die, and I told them so. I had nothing to lose.

Instead of pulling the trigger, thye pushed me over the rail. I fell thirty feet into the muddy river not known for giving up its victims.

I slid down through the water into the mud, but not so far, I couldn't kick myself free and push back up to the top before any water passed into my lungs. I lay on my right shoulder drifting as quietly as I could with the current. I did not look back to the bridge for what was above or below it.

The current took me under two more bridges and past the lights of the town and all human sound. The wet ropes loosened enough for me to slide one wrist out and then the other. I dog-paddled to the west side and floated along until my feet landed on a bank clear of underbrush. The steep hill took all my strength to climb, and I had to rest when I reached the top. The road that would bring me back to town was at least a quarter mile away.

I picked my way through the brush in the darkness following the sound of coal trucks driving north to Morgantown. Once I found the road, I scrambled along as best I could, but hid behind some rocks whenever a car drove by, figuring no one would be out this late unless they were looking for me.

Once the sun rose over the hills, I warmed up some and started walking faster. It was not unusual for others to be out this early and felt some comfort at not being alone. It took an hour to reach the town limits and by then, my clothes were nearly dry.

It was too early for the stores to open, which gave me the courage to look at myself in a plate glass window, knowing no one would be staring back. I didn't look bad enough to draw notice unless someone knew who I was. I weighed walking all the way through town and the eight miles south to my house or just going right over to see the sheriff. After some thought, I decided I didn't like either idea, so I crossed over the closest bridge to the east side of the river, walked down the streets until they ran out then followed the deer trails through the woods. In about an hour, I could see my bridge in a misty shadow waiting for the sun. There was no one on top and no one underneath. If you hadn't been there, you would have never known anything happened, giving rise to hoping it was all a dream or at least a mistake on my part. I climbed up the bank to my house and cleaned up.

After changing into dry clothes, I looked out my kitchen window and saw a state car parked in front of Bobby's. I called the Sheriff's office and asked to speak with him. He wasn't in, but they'd let him know I called. Ten minutes later I watched his car come over the bridge. I opened the front door and waited.

"You weren't here earlier," he said.

"No sir I was not."

"You know what's going on?"

"Yes sir. I think so." I explained what happened to Bobby and how they threw me over and how I floated down the river. He was glad I was okay and suggested someone had a powerful grudge against poor Bobby.

"The state police are investigating. Maybe they'll have an idea, though I can say for near certain, no one around here would take part in anything like this."

I make my living at cards, observing and remembering every detail, and provided the sheriff with a description of the three men, the make and model of the car and the license plate number. I don't remember things on purpose. It just comes naturally.

The sheriff shook his head, "That brain of yours is a wonder, that's for sure. Can I use your phone?" He dialed his office and asked them to call the state for the information on the car's owner.

"They'll call back. Got any coffee?"

He told me Corporal Silas of the state police was next door trying to coax information out of Bobby's wife. Everyone around here knew he was a bootlegger, but she probably wouldn't tell him that, meaning the corporal would come out knowing less than everyone else in town.

The phone rang, and the sheriff wrote down the name and address of the car owner.

"I'd stay out of Wheeling for while if I was you," he said.

I nodded. I knew Bobby sold there and said he lost a few customers but never knew why. The sheriff probably knew more about it than I did, but I wasn't going to ask.

"Know anything about who owned the car?"

"Michael Constantine. Petty theft, intimidation and running numbers."

"The syndicate?"

The sheriff nodded. "You best stay away."

"Yes sir," I said. "Either Bobby made a bad batch, or someone set him up."

"We may never know." He thanked me for the information and the coffee. Said he'd do his best to keep me out of it and walked out the door.

By the time the sheriff left, and I cleaned up the kitchen, it was close enough to noon that I drove to Russell's where those who could afford to buy lunch would be found.

"What'll you have?" I heard from behind the counter.

"You got that roast beef sandwich with mashed?"

"Sure. Want coffee?"

"Thanks."

Russell's filled up, and you could hear them whisper about poor Bobby.

Stan Lawson, owner of the pool hall, sat next to me. "You heard?"

"I heard."

"Damn shame. Moonshining comes to no good in the end, no matter how long it takes to catch up with you."

While Stan was talking, I remembered Bobby wasn't in business by himself. "What about Ike?" I said. "Think they got him?

Stan scowled. "Too mean to die if you ask me."

I almost mentioned Wheeling, but kept my mouth shut.

"We get a delivery on Fridays. We'll see if anyone comes by."

A year ago, Bobby showed me the mine shaft, and maybe I'll go up and take a look, or just tell the sheriff if he doesn't already know.

The pastor and the funeral director got together to give Bobby a proper send-off on Saturday morning, so anyone who wanted, could pay their respects. Bobby's sister, who we did not know, drove up from Elkins with her husband to attend. Ike escorted Bobby's wife to the front bench and sat with her during the service.

Well, at least Ike's alive.

Two weeks later I returned from Charlestown and decided to go find Bobby's still. I drove up the rutted road as far as the car would go and parked. I took my flashlight and walked the hundred yards to the mine. It was boarded up with a steel door attached to an oak frame that you could move to get inside. I slithered into pitch black. Even with the flashlight, all I could see was piles of rubble. No still. I walked another twenty feet to where the tunnel narrowed for the coal cars. There was no room for a still down there, and it wouldn't make sense anyway. They got Bobby and went and took his equipment.

I walked back to the entrance and out into the bright sunlight, then sat down and listened for a while. The only sound came from a light breeze moving through the trees and over to the slag pile where I was sitting.

Two months later, Corporal Silas announced they caught Bobby's killer. He was being held in Charlestown for trial. The man was identified as Anthony Carrillo from Wheeling, and they had his confession. Carrillo was not the name of the person who owned the car, and his picture did not look like any of the men I saw on the bridge. I heard that some men confess to crimes committed by others, so their families will be taken care of, and this may have been one of those cases, or he was being railroaded by the police to suit their purpose. A signed confession don't mean much if you didn't write it.

The corporal became a celebrity just in time to run for the County Sheriff's job, the one my uncle held for thirty years. When I told him I was sorry he lost, he said he should have retired before the election anyway, since his wife had passed away.

I saw Stan at the pool hall, and he told me moonshine was available again, but not from anyone he knew. Ike was seen with Bobby's wife a couple times, but no one knew the circumstances. Then one day, Ike's car was spotted in the airport parking lot. The sheriff confirmed that a man and woman looking like them boarded a plane to Washington DC, and no one's heard from them since.

A year later, a friend of mine told me he was going up to a game in Wheeling and did I want to come. I guessed enough time had passed and it would be safe, so I said yes.

Wheeling is a prosperous northern mill town on a sliver of West Virginia soil separating Ohio and Pennsylvania that holds little resemblance to the rest of the state that trails south down to Kentucky.

We drove around the city for a while to get our bearings then checked into a motel and found something to eat across the street. At ten, we walked into the bar and asked for Steve, who we were told could get us into the game. An older man came over and took us around the counter to an office and into a back room with two tables. They sat me at one and my buddy at another. They didn't know us and didn't want us to play off each other. I understood that.

The dealer called our attention. "This is a friendly game with no problems. You can leave any time. Game's over at five. If enough drop out, we'll make one table of who's left. House gets ten percent of the pot. If you have to be taken out of the room for any reason, your money stays on the table. Questions?" He introduced the two men who would make the rules stick, and I determined them to be big enough to do so.

While he was talking, another man came in and took the chair across from me. I paid no attention, keeping my eyes on the table.

An hour into the game the players settled into patterns I could read, except for the man facing me. He was betting when he didn't have the cards and getting upset when he lost. After a few more comments, the dealer asked if he'd like to take a break for a while and then come back. He shrugged it off and looked down at his cards.

After a few more hands he began to look familiar, so I kept my eyes off him, but he took notice of me for his own reasons and began to play more aggressively. I pulled back forfeiting a few chips, but that only seemed to increase his anger. He folded early in the next round, which allowed the rest of us to play without distraction.

The dealer gave me three Jacks and two eights, my best hand of the night. The other players were satisfied with their cards enough to keep bidding up the pot. The player across from me was leaning back and forth. In any other situation, he would have been an easy mark. He pushed all his chips onto the table. The other two players threw in their cards leaving me alone. I had no choice but to match his chips and call. He sat back with a smile on his face and did not move. The dealer asked him to continue.

"You first," the other man said," looking at me.

I looked at the dealer, who nodded. I spread my cards out on the table for everyone to see my full house.

"Your hand," said the dealer to the other player.

But he did not move. His face became bright red. It was clear he had the losing hand and was losing control of himself. I edged my chair back to get both feet on the floor but was unprepared for his next move. He picked up the edge of the table with both hands and threw it over to one side, grabbed a knife from his jacket, moved forward and sliced my left arm. I stepped back but tripped and fell to the floor. He came at me again, leaving me no choice but to defend myself the way I learned in the army. I rolled over onto my left shoulder and with my right arm reached around behind me for the gun in my waistband. I fired one shot into his heart. It is the easiest part of the body to hit when a man is charging at you. He fell backwards and lay silent on the floor.

I dropped my gun and handed my wallet to the bouncer, so he could see my permit to carry a weapon. The room was cleared. Someone wrapped a bandage around my arm and brought me to a second-floor office where I waited. Not much was said, and it took a while to quiet my nerves. Two men I hadn't seen before entered the room. They returned my wallet and my gun, unloaded. Fair enough.

One of them suggested I not return to Wheeling for a while and ushered me to the door. I recalled that wasn't the first time I'd received that advice.

Considering the police were never notified; unless it was the police who handed me my gun, I guessed the club was accustomed to handling their own problems.

My buddy was waiting downstairs with the car. We checked out of the motel and drove south to Morgantown where we stopped for breakfast.

"What do you think they did with the body?" I asked.

"Probably drove north and dropped it in the river."

"The Monongahela?"

"Yep. The River of Falling Banks, by God. With a little added weight, he'll bury in the mud. That don't bother you none, does it?"

"Can't say it does. No. Not at all."

We drove south under a clean sky with the first rays of sun reaching over the mountain peaks and splashing onto my window which I didn't mind at all and hardly noticed anyway cause I was thinking the muddy bottom of the Monongahela was a fitting end for the man who hanged my friend Bobby and threw me off the bridge into a river in which he would now be spending whatever time we had left in this world of ours.

WEST VIRGINIA 1955

The Reporter

John Stockman left his basement walkout four mornings a week to drive through a mile of single-family homes up college hill where he attended classes and studied in the library until the sun dropped behind the mountains across the river. He was one of seven- hundred-thousand students in the United States paying tuition, buying books, and taking classes with the hope of a good job the day they graduated. That he would be competing for work with younger men, he well understood. That he might soon die in an abandoned mineshaft never entered his mind.

At thirty-two, John was a World War II vet who'd kicked around Scranton for a while until a buddy suggested he use the G. I. Bill to get an education, unless he wanted to spend the rest of his life in a Lackawanna coal mine like his grandfather or the Lackawanna steel mill, where his father had eight years left to retire.

He attended college for two years before deciding to become a newspaper reporter, though taking classes in English and sociology was as close as he could get to a major in journalism. Most reporters of the day had a gift and honed their skills on the fly with the help of a seasoned editor.

Thursday nights, John sat in the only bar not occupied by the fraternities. Two friends from English 203 sat on the opposite side of a booth that always seemed to be empty when John arrived.

He took his first mouthful of beer, returned the glass to the table, and said "Good old three-point-two.

"Get to drink twice as much to get where you're going," said one of his friends.

"Only thing it's good for is chasing whiskey," said the other.

"The only thing you boys is good for is chasing the women I see you eyeing."

They gave him a thumbs-up.

John took another sip. "What are you writing on for your paper due next week?"

"They're digging up an old Indian campground in Monongah. I'll write about that," said one.

"Haven't decided," said the other.

"I'm gonna write about the bridges they built to get people back to work during the Depression," said John.

"Maybe you could sell that to the newspaper like that other one."

"I could," said John.

"You jumped out of a plane over Berlin. Why don't you write about that?"

John smiled. "I'll save that for my book. I like the bridges. Made it so people could get to the other side, and as you know, getting to the other side is very important these days."

"Here's to the other side."

John spent some time researching the bridges, and Monday morning, brought the outline to the editor, who was free with his thoughts; but said go ahead anyway.

"They needed those bridges," said the editor, "but it didn't bring the town together. Just seemed to make one side more wary of the other."

"I'd like to include something about the workers," said John.

"Write about the structure first, 'cause that's what everyone sees. Do you know how many tons of cement it took to build those bridges?"

"No."

"Me neither. But that will show the readers you know what you're writing about" The editor wrote a name and phone number on a piece of paper. "If you're interested in the people, here's someone you might talk to. His family's been living in this county as long as any. Say his family came in with Boone."

"Daniel Boone? I thought he was in Kentucky?"

"That's where he ended up, but he came through here first. Lived by Campbell's Creek till it got too crowded."

John returned to the library to look up the cubic yards of cement they used to build the bridge and the number of workers required to maintain a continuous pour. He found that most of the men who built it came from out of state and lived in shacks along the river, which did not put a lot of money in the pockets of the locals as they had hoped. Six workers fell to their death, five in the water and one in the mix. More than that died on the weekends of alcohol poisoning.

The first draft came together with little effort, and he had enough material for a follow-up story of a surveyor from Massachusetts who fell off the end of a flat bottom work boat with his transit and was never seen again. They informed his wife, who took the train down to see for herself. After being convinced her husband was gone, she took up with a foreman and stayed around till the job was done.

The following week, John turned in his English paper and the article for the newspaper. He figured he could compare comments made by his professor and the editor. At his age, he understood the need to learn as much as possible in the shortest period to keep him out of the mills unless it was for a story.

He received a B+ from his instructor and ten dollars from the editor.

John decided to begin work on the follow-up piece. He looked at the slip of paper the editor gave him and called the number. Mathew Mansfield answered on the second ring.

John drove his '53 Jeep across the four lane WPA cement bridge to East Fairmont and out East Grafton Road past the cemetery, down Burnt Cabin until it narrowed to a one-lane wooden bridge and a gravel road with a sign warning that the state road ends here. A half-mile further, he veered right, down a path to the bottom of a ravine then back up a drive to the top of the hill, past a vegetable garden and, thank God, finally into Mr. Mansfield's front yard.

The bungalow style house, with a half dormer and porch that took advantage of the setting sun, was painted off-white, including trim boards. The yard was cleaner than most John had seen. A one-car garage with raised door stood off to the left. A green Ford pickup rested inside. The screen door opened and closed.

"Heard you coming," said Mathew, who stood solid, broad-shouldered and muscular, an inch below six feet, strong hands, short gray hair, tanned face and neck, soft hazel eyes that never got around to turning blue that reflected the past but were clear enough to see the sins of those who stood before him.

When Mathew was a boy, he ranged the back woods with a young native they called "The Indian," who was the last of a small band that roamed the forests a thousand years before the Seneca and other tribes took up the forests east of the Ohio River. Mathew and The Indian held an easy truce, preserved by their knowledge of a common enemy who took the land for profit and brought despair to those who came before.

"Afternoon. I'm John Stockman," He walked up the steps and held out his hand.

"You're a little old to be in college."

John smiled. "GI Bill. Had to do some work for Uncle Sam first."

"In the war?"

"Hundred and First."

Mathew looked down at the porch floorboards. "My son was in the third division. Killed on Salerno Beach, September 3rd. 1943."

"I'm sorry. I lost my best friend when we jumped over Utah Beach. He was gone before we hit the ground."

"Well, it's over. Want a beer?"

Mathew returned with two beers, pointed to a chair for John and then sat in a wooden rocker that had borne his weight through crises and grief: the loss of his son and years later, the loss of his wife.

From the porch, John looked down the hill through the trees that thinned to a long view of the gravel road, back to the bridge. Though he wasn't sure how much of this land belonged to Mathew, he guessed that all of it had belonged to his ancestors at one time or the other.

Off to the side, the sun fell on a large vegetable garden with neat rows of beans, squash, tomatoes, corn, and potatoes. Between the house and the garage, a raised bed of flowers was in full bloom.

"That bed belonged to my wife."

"A woman's touch," said John.

Mathew nodded. "You said on the phone you were writing for the newspaper."

"It's a follow-up story."

"Why is it newspapers don't get their facts straight?"

"You noticed that too? Problem is, most people don't get their facts straight, and we just report what they tell us."

"Well, I'll tell you this. Truth is, most people don't know that much, including they don't know that they don't know what they think they know."

John laughed. "You're right about that, but I guess they got to put something in between the ads."

"Why do you want to be a reporter, anyway? Seems like all they do is nose around other people's business."

"Nosing around is a good way to keep people honest; same as the law, except we get to print what we find. The editor said your family lived here as long as anyone. I wrote a story about the three bridges in town and wanted to learn about the people back when they were built."

"Three bridges? We got five. There's one north on the way to Morgantown, by the city limits. Then there's one south that's one-lane over the river to Railroad Town. Trains use to stop for water years ago, but not anymore."

"Got a name?"

"Not really. Some call it Hanging Bridge."

"Vigilantes?"

"You could say that."

"How far out of town?" John wrote down five miles.

Mathew told him there was a man who lived in the first house on the left as you crossed the bridge, if he cared to learn more.

"What was it like here during the Depression?"

"People here were farmers and worked in the mines. It was always hard. Depression just made it worse."

"WPA help?"

"They built bridges, roads, and a nice park seven miles out of town. Nothing changed except we got roads, bridges and a park nobody could get to 'cause there was no money for gas."

"Coal mines?"

"Small ones closed. They couldn't compete with the big ones, an' even some of them are gone."

"Any around anywhere?"

"Closest is Farmington twelve miles up Route 50 if you want to see one. Goes down three-hundred feet; though they say it's too deep, and someday the gases will explode it to Hell and back. Course getting coal was never the problem. The problem was getting someone to buy it at a price worth getting it out of the ground in the first place."

John stood up and put his pad away. "I've got a lot to learn. Would you mind if I stop back sometime?"

"Stop by any time."

After saying goodbye, he drove carefully down the driveway onto the gravel road. He looked back through his rear-view mirror to make sure he hadn't run over anything. He didn't relax until he was over the bridge, and his tires were on solid pavement.

Back at the library, John used microfiche to search the newspaper for the bridge-hanging incident. He was surprised to learn that the victim had been cut down by Sheriff Mathew Mansfield.

The next day class ended at 2:30. John threw his bag in the back of the Jeep and drove off campus down the west side of the river. He traveled this road before but never noticed a bridge. In fact, the woods were so thick you couldn't see the river. John watched the odometer tick off eight miles before he doubled back. Three miles later, he saw a narrow dirt road behind a row of trees that blocked its view from the north. John turned down the hill, around a bend and found himself on a wooden bridge before he could stop.

He drove past the row of houses to the railroad track that ran north and south with nothing on the other side except an abandoned water tower and an overgrown dirt road that lead to nowhere in particular. He turned the Jeep around and drove back, stopping in front of the house closest to the river. Before he stepped out of his jeep, the door opened. A thin man of average height wearing glasses stood on the porch.

"Pennsylvania. Saw you drive over the bridge."

"Hi. I'm down here for college. I was talking to Mr. Mansfield an' he told me to stop by if I wanted to learn about the bridge."

"Mathew did call me."

"Told me they found a man underneath, though he didn't tell me he was the one who cut him down and he didn't tell me he was the sheriff back then either. My name is John."

"I'm Savo. You're a little old to be in college, ain't you?"

"I keep hearing that. I was in the war."

"Me too. You talk to Mathew about that?"

"Said he lost his son."

"We were at Salerno together moving up the beach under heavy fire. We crawled forward as fast as we could until Tommy stopped moving. It was a hell of a thing."

"War's a hell of a thing."

"A hell of thing, all right."

The conversation ended. All that was left was to shift weight until one of them changed the subject, so they could start over.

"You know the man who was hanged?"

Savo looked at the house next to his. "Lived right there. Bobby Thompson. A friend of mine. He was selling moonshine, and somebody took to disliking him for it. Brought his wife down to the river and made her watch."

"My God, that was awful."

"Yes, it was."

"I'm sorry. Prohibition's over. Who buys moonshine?"

"Lots of people. You get a good feeling when it goes down and a better feeling knowing the government ain't getting your money."

"Great endorsement. Where was the still? Across the tracks?

"Way across. Up in the hills in a mine owned by his partner, Ike."

"What happened to him?"

"His partner and his wife were last seen getting on a plane to Washington, at least that's where they found the car."

"Sheriff get who killed Bobby?"

"No. State trooper, named Silas, then he ran for sheriff after that, and that's who we got today."

"Would you show me the mine?"

"I'm going on the road for a couple of days. Be back next Tuesday. If you want, I'll take you up then."

"Okay. What do you do, anyway?"

"I'll show you. Play cards?"

"A little."

Savo led him inside the house, which was neater and cleaner than John had expected for a single man. Sitting at the kitchen table, Savo handed him a deck of cards.

"Shuffle 'em up anyway you want an' deal."

John turned the cards over several times then dealt two hands for five-card draw. After losing nine straight, he gave up. Savo told him not to be discouraged. First, John had a run of bad luck, then Savo a run of good luck, but even if that were not the case, Savo would have won because that was what he did for a living. John put the cards away, shaking his head. "I guess this ain't my game against you."

Walking to his Jeep, he eyed the bridge. "Mind if I go down and take a look?"

"I'll wait up here."

From the river's edge, he looked up at the rusty girders supporting the oak timbers laid a quarter inch apart and tried to picture a man hanging at the end of a rope. He was glad that he could not. But for some reason he could picture Bobby's wife watching her husband fall until the rope caught up and snapped his neck, becoming a silhouette hanging in the dark above the slow-moving water.

That evening, John stopped by a local diner for a quick meal. The waitress, who appeared to be in her fifties and might have worked there most of her life, took his order for a corned beef and a basket of fries. To test the local knowledge, he asked if she knew anything about an old mine where they made moonshine. She looked at John and paused before giving her reply. "You could ask the sheriff over there about that, if you want."

John nodded and looked over. He thought it best not to let on he was interested in exploring someone else's private property.

Next Tuesday, John picked up Savo who directed him over the railroad track to the back roads that were once used by coal trucks to pick up their loads until the mine shut down when there was no one left to dig out what little coal was left.

The only other vehicle they saw was a deputy's' car, which occurred to John to be a little unusual when there was nothing out here except back woods and empty fields. Savo pointed to the left, and John veered off to another dirt road that climbed a small hill then took a second rise until it ended where boulders blocked the road.

"Can you make it up any further in this thing?"

John engaged his lowest gear and crawled over and around rocks and gravel until he reached the mine's entrance.

"Number nine," said Savo.

"There's nothing here."

"Never was much to begin with. These guys are wildcatters. They lease the equipment, dig a tunnel into the mountain, take what's there, an' leave. No insurance, low wages and too small for anyone to take notice. If they go bust, they start another company."

The entrance was closed with a steel door attached to a heavy oak frame, bolted into the rock. Two-by-fours were nailed up on the left side where the frame wasn't square.

"Shine your light in there," said Savo.

John squinted into the darkness with his right eye and played the flashlight through a hole just below his shoulder. He could see piles of debris. "A little cramped in there."

"They blow up the entrance with a stick of dynamite to discourage trespassers."

"This the mine where Bobby kept his still? asked John.

"Yeah. This was Ike's alright. After shutting it down he made more money in moonshine than coal."

"So, if Ike flew off somewhere, where'd the equipment go?"

" Somebody's got it, cause you can still get moonshine."

John gave up trying to see anything and followed Savo back outside. "How come Ike and Bobby worked together?"

"They were cousins; not close cousins, just convenient cousins."

"This the only shaft in the mountain?"

"The only one I know about."

"If there was another around here, where'd it be?"

Savo pointed south past the mine. "The shaft would most likely be around the mountain in that direction."

"Mountain's not that big. Let's take a look."

They left the Jeep and scrambled over piles of shale and debris near impossible to walk over.

"We're fighting the mine rubble. Should be easier ahead."

Soon, the ground leveled off, and they came to an overgrown path that should not have been there. They walked slower, listening for anyone nearby. Twenty minutes later, voices carried up the hillside. They waited but didn't hear them again. Savo pointed into the woods and once again, they were working their way around trees and mountain holly.

Savo reached the ledge first. Twenty feet below, they saw a gravel pit and a dirt road leading back down the mountain. A faded blue pickup truck loaded with propane tanks was parked off to the left. A minute later, two men walked out of the mine. Savo looked at John and motioned downward with his finger. They lay quiet until the men drove away.

John and Savo moved back along the trail through the woods and over the rubble to reach the Jeep. John put it in low and drove back around the boulders onto the gravel road and down the mountain. Unspoken was the fear that they had been spotted and the blue pickup would be waiting for them somewhere below.

A half-hour later, John drove into Savo's front yard. They looked for a pickup, but none came by.

"Think Mathew knows about the mine?"

"Don't know."

"Should we tell him?"

Savo called Mathew who invited them up for a meal.

"You had some excitement," said Mathew.

Savo looked up. "They had a truck full of tanks an' drove off."

"You found the still, I expect," said Mathew.

"So, Ike's back in business?" asked John.

"Maybe, but if they think they've been found out, they'll just move on."

"If it's Bobby's, we should go up there," said Savo.

"An' get your head shot off."

"Then what?" asked Savo

"I suspect they know you were up there and let you off. If you went back you'd find them gone. Either way, you don't have to worry about it. Who wants another pork chop?"

John never needed an alarm clock to wake up in the morning. Whatever time he wanted to get up, he just woke up, sometimes before, but never later; and if he didn't need to get up, the first light of dawn brought him to consciousness whether he liked it or not. Next morning, early, he drove his Jeep up the gravel road and parked at the entrance of the old mine. After grabbing his camera and flashlight, he retraced his steps to the ledge overlooking the mineshaft. With no truck in sight or voices from below, he climbed down the hill to the entrance.

It wasn't long before he found the still, and wooden crates full of empty bottles. Walking deeper into the mine, all he could see was his beam of light dissolving into darkness and black walls. He looked back to the sun lit entrance growing smaller with every step.

He was about to go back when he felt a brush of cool air. He turned only to see the flashlight's beam swallowed up in the darkness of another mineshaft. He stepped through the narrow entrance shining his light in all directions. The tunnel sloped downward to depths he had no intention of exploring. He swept the walls with his light until he saw a small opening with two skeletons inside covered with dust. As gruesome as this might be for others, it was no match for his war experience. He knelt down for a closer look. By sifting through the bones and the dirt, he found a man's wallet.

John returned to the main shaft where he took pictures of the still before walking outside into the blinding daylight and didn't see the four-wheel-drive by the storage shed or the driver next to the truck.

"Find what you're looking for?"

With the sun in his eyes, John could barely see the outline of a man holding a rifle.

"I'll take that camera. Now turn around and walk back inside."

"I'm not alone, you know."

"I been watching you since you got here. You're alone."

John looked down at the ground to get the sun out of his eyes.

"Thought you'd come here and cause trouble, did you? Get inside, I said."

John could only think he'd be joining the two skeletons in the mineshaft. "You got my camera, so let me go."

"You ain't going nowhere."

Before he turned around, a second man, whose features he could not make out, walked up behind the man with the rifle.

"Put down that rifle, Silas."

Silas turned around. "Why Mathew, what are you doing here?"

"Taking care of unfinished business."

"Well, I caught this nosey out-of-state fella trespassing on private property."

"Terrible thing that. A man ought to have more respect. But he's one of those reporter types and don't know better, I suspect."

"I'm going to arrest him and charge him with a felony."

"Not today, Silas. You're the one that's getting arrested."

"You can't arrest me. I'm the sheriff."

"Well, I guess I knew that, so I brought some of your old state trooper friends along to do it for me."

Mathew took the rifle while the troopers handcuffed the sheriff, then looked at John. "You are an early riser, Mr. Stockman."

"Not as early as you, Mr. Mansfield. Remember, people thought Ike and Bobby's wife left town?" John handed Mathew the wallet. "Their bodies are back in the mine."

Mathew looked through the wallet and gave John an appreciative nod. "Well now," he said with a grin on his face, "writing a story about a sheriff and his deputies doing life up in Moundsville for two murders while running a still, sure beats that one you wrote about those three bridges, don't it?"

Restitution

In 1955, Congress voted to replace the *E Pluribus Unum* printed on the founding fathers' Great Seal of the United States with the words *In God We Trust*, returning confidence and equilibrium to those who considered this revision necessary to preserve our union. In December of that same year, police arrested Rosa Parks for refusing to give up her seat to a white man on the Cleveland Avenue bus in Montgomery, creating anger and anxiety on both sides of that great divide, scattering that new-found equilibrium to the wind. Both events generated enough news and opinions to fill a newspaper for months to come without an ounce of heft.

Nevertheless, on a late Friday night, the managing editor of Morgantown's only newspaper, The New Dominion, was working overtime, and laughing when he created the headline QUARTER MILLION DISAPPEARS FROM STATE BANK for his Saturday edition. The bank that lost the money lay sixteen miles south in another town where a competing newspaper was attempting to downplay the troubles of its mortgage holder. *That'll show 'em down there how to run a newspaper*, he said to himself.

Everyone had theories, of course. Money doesn't vanish. It was an inside job. Lucky thieves were in way over their heads, or the money had been siphoned off over the years with the short fall now being passed along to the FDIC. Sure, they arrested someone driving the getaway car. They even found a dead robber, so they said; even though the money was still missing and not everyone was accounted for, leaving the equation seriously out of balance.

Joseph Ryder parked his brother's three-year-old '56, light green, four-door Ford sedan on Main Street next to a used furniture store, with dirty windows, that sold dented bookcases, rusted ironing boards and stained couches. He walked down the hill alongside the building to the River Edge bar. Not long ago, it had lost half its customers to the larger clubs that added pool tables, dance floors and Saturday night bands. Now, the usuals were those who either shouldn't be drinking or didn't want to be seen. There was always an empty stool, and at least one open booth for the taking.

River Edge rested on the ground floor of the town's oldest brick building. The front door looked out to the west bank of the north-flowing Monongahela River. No one went in by mistake or uninvited except the river, when the waters floods over its banks to disgorge the excessive spring rains that pummeled the county most every year that people could remember.

Sitting in the booth with his back to the wall, Ryder faced Walter, his accountant friend, and Natchez, his Indian friend. They ordered each a bottle of Rolling Rock, which was Pennsylvania's contribution to the short list of beers available in a state that forgot prohibition had ended twenty-six years ago.

Walter asked Ryder what was on everyone's mind. "What time you leaving tomorrow?"

"Round noon, I guess. Its two hours away, an' they're not gonna let him out 'till three."

"What's he gonna do?"

"Ain't gonna do nothing," said Natches, "least ways not 'round here. They don't hire ex-cons, they don't hire Indians, an' if there were any blacks, they wouldn't hire them neither."

"He never did nothing," said John, "and is, therefore, not an ex-con. If Mansfield had been reelected sheriff, my brother would not of gone to prison."

"They said he drove the get-away car."

"You think he'd rob a bank and drive away in car that everybody knows? I'll give you it was his car, but he wasn't in it."

"You still think it was the Pritchett's?" asked Walter.

"Who else you know who'd do it? They killed Jeremy, too. I ain't saying my little brother was an angel, but he didn't deserve to die."

"Well, they sure ain't spent the money. It's been three years, and they're living like hogs scavenging off an empty cornfield," said Walter.

"They're waiting," said Natchez. "I see 'em waiting."

Natchez was the nephew of The Indian. No white man knew the Indian's real name, and he didn't care to advance their learning. His great-grandfather was a sachem whose people roamed the mountains hundreds of years before Boone led the English and the Scots into the Appalachians to start up new lives. Of course, they didn't always get their way. More than once the Indians took their guns and furs and sent them scurrying back to their cabins empty-handed. But most of the time it was the other way.

Natchez spoke of these times without conceding to the memories of harsh treatment burning inside. He displayed no ill will and sat patiently, even while being kicked around by the whites whenever their personal failings were more than they could bear. He made do by moving boxes in a small warehouse off the highway, sleeping in his uncle's cabin and hiking the forests wondering what it must have been like before corn whiskey, clear cutting and strip mining.

While Natchez, born in the Appalachian Mountains, whose grandparents were the last to have access to its bounties, was a link to the past, Walter, a bookkeeper with a mind for balancing financial accounts, was a harbinger of the future; and neither fit in with the present.

Walter was slim, average height, nearsighted, introverted, and a graduate of a local college accounting program. He worked in the back office of the bank that had lost half its holdings on a Tuesday morning in October, but he had been moved into the new branch office two days before the robbery, leaving him absent during the crime and absent of any inside information that might be useful. Walter was the first to admit, by luck or by chance, he was never around when anything happened and always the last to know if it did.

One of Walter's jobs was to balance the cashiers' accounts at the end of the day. On a few occasions, he helped the young tellers balance their tally sheets by redistributing a few dollars; but as often as he provided these favors, to his great disappointment, none were ever returned.

On the day the bank began the transfer of a half million dollars to their new branch, two men wearing long coats and masks took half the money then jumped into the back seat of a waiting car that drove down main street and out of town. Whether the men were in a hurry, or inexperienced for taking only half the money, no one knew, but clearly, they were amateurs failing to maximize financial gain for the effort they put into their work.

Until the police found $450 of the bank's money under the back seat of John Ryder's light green ford and his younger brother, Jeremy, face down on the side of the road ten miles out of town, with a bullet in his head, they hadn't dug up one clue or even formed a suspect list.

A passing motorist called in the body, but who called in John's light green Ford was anybody's guess. It wasn't long before he was locked up for three years, and his brother placed in the ground forever.

The parents, long dead from a trucking accident, had a thing for the letter "J," giving each child a first name beginning with the tenth letter of the alphabet. Their daughter, Jill, had long ago moved to Ohio. She married a factory worker in Akron and had no intention of returning to the "Hills" as she called her Appalachian roots. Joseph was happy for her, but never understood why anyone would want to live in a city. He spent four years in the Army to learn a trade but found he would have to live north of Reno for a career in tank repair.

Fortunately, Joseph was at Fort Bragg when the robbery took place driving a beat-up Half-Track through a swamp to collect a platoon stranded during a night exercise, or more than likely the police would have charged him as well, and he'd be sitting in prison with his brother.

Unfortunately, he was at Fort Bragg when the robbery took place and was unable to prevent this tragedy from happening in the first place.

The city's first-ever detective had the case wrapped up by the next weekend and submitted his written report before the new chief arrived for his first day of work that Monday morning. The detective constructed a textbook theory of the crime then jammed the evidence in sideways to make it fit. His theory sent an innocent man to prison, and as is always the case in these circumstances, allowed the guilty to go free.

The report said John Ryder had been driving the get-away car while his younger brother, Jeremy, and an unknown third party robbed the bank. John drove them to a second vehicle and returned home. Later, Jeremy Ryder and the third party got into a dispute over the money and the third party shot and killed Jeremy. The third party was still at large, and no one could explain why John Ryder would not identify the person who killed his brother. That John was innocent, and did not know who pulled the trigger, never entered the detective's mind.

Sheriff Mansfield had lost the election, and the new sheriff left the investigation to the young detective without question or oversight. John was found guilty of driving the get-away car and sentenced to seven years in the state penitentiary up in Moundsville. His time would be reduced to three and a half for good behavior and because the prison was overcrowded.

Joseph slid out of the booth and walked to the bar where a small black-and-white TV was broadcasting the fourth game of the World Series.

"Who's winning?"

"Dodgers. Doesn't look good for the White Sox."

"Don't follow it much."

"Your brother did. He knew every team and most players. Think they let him watch the game up there?"

"Probably not."

Three new bottles were opened and placed on the bar. Joseph returned to the booth with the second round. They had covered this ground before, but he couldn't help bringing it up again.

"The day the money was to be moved, two people just happened to be standing there in masks and drove away with a quarter million, leaving the other half behind." He took his first swallow from the fresh bottle and shook his head. "Who'd those Pritchett boys know at the bank?"

Walter remained burdened with undeserved guilt for not having the information he felt was his responsibility to uncover. He didn't know any more than anyone else nor was he even aware of the rumors circulating about town. "I don't know." he said. "I wish I did."

"Did they know any tellers?"

"Maybe," said Walter, "but they didn't know the money was being moved until just before the truck was to arrive."

"Somebody knew something," said Natchez. "What about the driver?"

"They just follow a schedule. They don't know what they're picking up until they get there."

"Makes no difference how they did it," said Natchez. "If you believe the Pritchett's did it, go see 'em."

"An' what? They ain't gonna show me where they hid the money, and they sure ain't gonna admit they killed my brother."

"After three years, who knows what they'll do. Maybe they're getting tired of waiting," said Natchez

Joseph raised the bottle to his lips, took another sip and leaned forward. "I'd sure like to know who they're waiting for, and if they did shoot my brother, they'd think nothing of shooting me."

"Maybe," said Natchez. He waited a few seconds and continued. "There is a story of white men riding into an Indian camp when the warriors were away. They killed the elders and stole the horses. When the warriors returned, one of them followed their trail to the river. He followed the river to a trading post and saw the horses tied outside a barn. That night he went inside and found two men sleeping. He tied them up, then returned to the village with the horses."

"That really happen?" asked Walter.

"That's the story," said Natchez.

"What was your tribe?" asked Joseph.

"No tribe."

"What do you mean no tribe?"

"We lived here before the tribes. The Saponi came later, but there were not many, and we were friends. Later the Iroquois and Shawnee came and took our land, so we moved into the forest. Then the white man came an' cut down our trees. The earth dried up and burst into flame. Now there are only rocks shaped by the winds to remind us of our ancestors and our gods."

"How many gods did you have?"

"A lot more than we have now."

"I know that forest," said Walter. "Government blowed it to hell during training exercises and left sixty-millimeter live rounds on the ground. More than one hunter got carried out in a bag."

"And you thought it was only the Indians the government don't care about," said Natchez with a smile.

Walter turned to Natchez. "That the end of the story?"

"They buried their dead and waited. Two days later, five men rode up the trail to the Indian camp. The warriors hid behind trees and called out their names as they rode by. The white men became angry and charged into the woods after them. When it was over, the white men were buried and the camp moved on."

"Do you have any stories where people live happily ever after?" asked Walter.

"They killed the elders," Natchez reminded him.

Walter lifted his bottle of beer. "To retribution."

Joseph pointed his bottle at Natchez. "To retribution. Now tell me, how'd the Indian know their names?"

Natchez leaned forward. "In the barn, he told the two men whoever tells him who stole the horses would live."

"He killed them?" said Walter.

"Only one, but he left them tied together so the other wouldn't forget."

Joseph finished his beer and placed the empty on the table. He leaned over to Natchez. "What are you telling me?"

"Nothing, It's just a story."

Joseph stood up from the booth and threw some money on the table. "Got to get up early."

The next morning Joseph rummaged through his footlocker until he found what he was looking for. On his way out the door, he grabbed his father's old double- barrel shotgun and put it in the trunk of his brother's car.

He drove straight to the Pritchett family house and parked behind the pickup truck, just as the sun's first rays filtered through the willow branches and glinted off the kitchen window. He laid on the horn and waited. A few minutes later, the older boy, Samuel, pushed open the screen door and walked onto the small porch. He shielded his eyes from the sun until he recognized the car.

"That you Joseph?"

"Yeah. Got something for you."

"What're doing out here so early? Thought you'd be heading up to Moundsville. Today's the day, ain't it?"

"Today's the day. Where's your brother, Tommy? Got something for him too."

Samuel pulled up his shirt to show the pistol in his waistband. "You ain't here to cause trouble, are you? I got my gun right here."

A minute later, Tommy came through the screen door with a small-bore shotgun, his eyes on Joseph, who was sitting with his hands on the steering wheel. When Tommy reached the car window, Joseph handed him the keys. "Here, open the trunk."

Tommy didn't like to be told what to do, but he walked back and looked inside.

"What's that old double barrel for?"

"Take a closer look."

Both boys had their heads half in the trunk looking at that shotgun when Joseph slipped out of the drivers' seat and walked up behind them pointing a Smith and Wesson at the youngest brother.

"Tommy, put your bird gun in the trunk; and you, Samuel, take out your pistol and throw it in the trunk too, so I don't have to take your brother's head off."

Joseph looked down at Samuel's handgun. "What've you got there? Just an old Browning, 22-target pistol. Not much of a gun, but enough to put a bullet into someone's head." Joseph closed the trunk and pointed his gun at the brothers. "Now my Smith and Wesson's a real gun, a .38 Chief's Special. A friend of mine gave it to me after he retired. Said it might come in handy. Guess he was right. Let's walk up behind your house to that tree line."

When the brothers reached the scrub oak, they turned around.

"Now," said Joseph, "you're gonna tell me what you did with that money you stole."

Samuel gave Ryder a hard look. "That was your brother who stole the money."

"I don't think so," said Joseph. He took careful aim, pulled the trigger and placed a bullet into Samuel's right leg, bringing him to the ground. There was a lot of blood and a lot more pain.

"You don't have much of time before you bleed out, so this is what's gonna happen. One of you will tell me where you hid the money and the other goes to his grave like my brother."

"And which of us would that be?" asked the little brother.

"Makes no difference to me," said Joseph. "Whoever wants to bury the other, I guess." He took three steps backward and raised his gun. "After what you did, you can't tell me you didn't see this coming."

Joseph drove the Ford out of the driveway with two bags of money in the trunk of his brother's car. He followed the narrow road until he reached Route 250, which wandered northwest alongside a thin strip of river that grew from a convergence of creeks with names like Drake Run and Clear Drain, creeks that meandered slowly along their banks until flash floods turned them into furies no man could abide.

He drove north dodging the forty-five-ton double-axel coal trucks barreling toward him at breakneck speed taking one-and-a half-lanes and kicking up enough of the dirt and gravel to create whirlwinds in their wake. And when one would come up from behind, he would pull over and let it pass, though there were few areas wide enough where the road cut between shale and limestone deposited long before the ocean receded back to become the Mississippi River.

Joseph reached the middle span of the bridge crossing the Monongahela and pulled over. He opened the trunk and dropped both shotguns into the river below.

He continued north where he'd see an occasional piece of cleared land with a single house sitting next to a garden of sunflowers and peas looking as peaceful as any hillside could be on a warm, sunny day. But he did wonder who would live so far from town, and what they gained from their experience.

Joseph reached the center of Moundsville and followed First Street until turning left on Jefferson where he drove slowly by the most imposing and frightening Gothic fortress ever designed. The state penitentiary was a medieval castle with turrets and battlements, except theses parapets were armed with machine guns. The stonewalls, more than five-feet thick at the base, contained within, years of brutality and amusement for the persecutors.

The public could attend hangings until one inmate was decapitated. After that, viewings required the warden's invitation, which were easy to come by if you were interested. For a while, the penitentiary had been included in the list of top ten most violent correctional facilities in the United States, and Joseph had feared that his brother would not make it out alive.

He filled his tank at the first gas station he saw, having long ago given up brand allegiance when Sunoco started buying up the independents. He found a post office and purchased a cardboard mailer large enough to hold the Browning, 22. He addressed the box to the Marion County State Police Barracks, inserted the handgun, and enclosed a written note suggesting the gun was used to kill Jeremy Ryder.

Joseph pulled into the parking lot of the state penitentiary and walked to the visitor's entrance. After picking up a clipboard and signing his name, he was allowed into a small room with a wooden bench pressed against the wall. The door closed, and he was left alone. He wondered if he would have been able to survive even these conditions.

A few minutes later a buzzer rang, and a small metal door opened. He stood up and watched his brother, dressed in civilian clothes for the first time in three years, walk into the room. Joseph did not move. He wanted to see that John wasn't bound or restrained in any way. He wanted to see his brother unshackled and free to walk out alone.

They stood at the exit, waiting for the door to open. Neither looked at the guard behind the bulletproof glass or looked back at the imposing exterior walls as they walked to the car.

Joseph backed out onto Jefferson and drove north for two hours until they reached Pittsburgh. He stopped at a used car lot, and for much less than it was worth, sold the light-green Ford with the understanding that the salesman would give them a ride to the bus station, so they could be in Washington DC, by morning. Joseph bought two one-way bus tickets to the nation's capital, but the brothers got off when it stopped to pick up passengers at the airport.

"They let you watch any of the Series?

"Not much."

"With any luck we'll catch the fifth game at Comiskey Park. Who do you like, the Dodgers or the White Sox?"

"I don't care. I just like to watch the game."

They bought two tickets to Chicago, two cups of coffee and waited for the American Airlines flight #386 with two-hundred and fifty-thousand dollars in two bags sitting on the floor between them.

"What are we gonna do when we get back?" asked John.

"Ain't going back," said Joseph. "Ain't no going back at all. We got what they said you stole and you did your time, which ties the score so far as I can see."

"What about our younger brother, Jeremy?"

"That score got tied up before you ate breakfast this morning.

West Virginia 1961

The Last Foxhole

There is no experience that induces the feeling of helplessness and the acceptance of fate more than lying in a foxhole listening to the sound of enemy bullets slamming into the ground around you, the sound of mortar explosions bursting your ear drums and the sight of men being killed as fast as you can blink your eyes in disbelief

"Stout!" shouted the sergeant, "We need more ammo."

Corporal Stout scrambled out of the foxhole and ran as fast as he could, bent over, head down, holding on to his helmet until he reached a supply truck two hundred yards behind their lines. He rested for three minutes to catch his breath, picked up six belts of ammunition, each weighing ten pounds, and ran back in the same manner, stooped over, looking up occasionally to get his bearings, until another soldier tackled him.

"They're gone," yelled the soldier.

"What?"

"They're gone," he yelled over the sounds of explosions shattering the air around them.

Stout looked over to his foxhole and saw three bodies lying on the ground.

"A direct hit," yelled the soldier. "You're lucky you weren't there."

Stout sat up and released the ammunition belts. He could not keep his eyes off those men and did not move until someone pulled him down into a foxhole. He lay on his back listening to the shells fly overhead and explode around him. In his mind, those soldiers rose up and walked off the battlefield until they were out of sight. He wished that he were with them.

After all the foxholes had been destroyed by enemy fire, and he was the last man in his company left alive, they sent him to the rear one more time where, following a quick check by a medic, was ordered to remain until the war was over.

I met Corporal Stout fourteen years later, with his head down working on a project in the basement of his home where he spent every evening after finishing a light dinner of meat and vegetables. He kept his head down until he turned off the basement light and walked up two flights of stairs to bed where his wife had been sleeping for the last hour, often with a wet facecloth over her forehead to ward off a migraine headache.

I had transferred from one college to another in a different city and rented the first room I could find as I was in a hurry, though I could not have been more pleased with my surroundings. The house felt immediately comfortable, and the distance to the college was less than a mile away.

The living room in this small home was full of Early American and Victorian antique furniture, and though there was nothing from the more expensive Empire or Federal periods, the room was inviting, nonetheless. For reasons unknown to me, I preferred music from my parents' generation over my own, radio broadcasts over black-and-white television, and, of course, Early American and Victorian furniture that had been pulled from the mist of time.

One warm October afternoon, I returned to the house after class and noticed an empty space in the living room, then realized a couch was missing. My imagination took over and I wondered what would be gone when I returned from school tomorrow? Was it possible that I might come back to an empty home? I quickly went upstairs to see if I still had a bed to sleep on.

When I heard Mrs. Stout enter the house through the kitchen door, I came downstairs to say hello. After a few minutes of conversation, I brought myself to ask about the missing couch.

"I sold it," she said, "and did very well."

"You sell your furniture?" I asked.

"Yes. Everything here is for sale, except the children of course. Although some days..."

She wandered off point and took a minute to return.

"I sell the antique furniture in my house, from my house. It's cheaper than owning a store, and it gives us something to sit on, which you'll have to agree, is more comfortable than the alternative."

I don't remember whether she twirled around the living room while speaking, but I would not have been surprised if she had.

"We have more couches in the garage, with matching end tables if you're interested. When my husband comes home, we'll move another one into the living room."

"How long have you been doing this?" I asked.

"Since my grandmother died and left me her furniture. Everything she collected over the years ended up in our garage."

The garage, which I had no reason to notice and could have belonged to anyone, sat on the other side of a narrow lane that ran between several homes. This would have been an alley in a city, but here you could see the sun and walk on grass indented with tire tracks.

"Will you be home tonight?" she asked.

"Yes."

"Then, we'll have a party. The four of us."

The four would be, I came to understand, Mrs. Stout, her two children and myself, as Mr. Stout spent his evenings in the basement with his projects.

Willie, the youngest in the family, was a likable, skinny fifth-grade student. He wore a crew cut and black rimmed glasses. For the record, the frames of my glasses were brown. His sister, Annie, a seventh-grade student, was also thin. She resembled her mother in looks with blond hair, sunken cheeks and narrow nose. She was keenly aware of others, and quick to respond if the opportunity arose, but remained in the background while her mother played hostess with a measure of flamboyance ever on display, knowing that at any moment someone could walk through the front door and be her next customer.

I remember most that she was a proud Republican in a Democratic state. Every week the mailman delivered her Time Magazine, a bastion of Republican idealism back then, which no one could touch until she read every word, cover-to-cover. I never did discover where the old magazines were stored after the next one dropped through the mail slot. Mrs. Stout was also a member of the Women's Republican Party, writing letters and contributing to discussion groups at every opportunity. When a Catholic was elected President of the United States, there were enough tears to flood the creek over its banks.

The family had finished dinner by the time I returned from campus. By eight, we assembled in the living room around a card table. As I suspected, Mr. Stout did not join us. Mrs. Stout explained that he had a long day, and what we were about to do required a lot of energy.

At the age of twenty, I had plenty to give and looked forward to the adventure, though I had no idea what that would be.

"This is a good night," announced Mrs. Stout. "I can feel it."

The two children were excited and placed their hands face down on the table. Mrs. Stout motioned for me to do the same. With a bit more ceremony, she placed her hands on the table, palms down, and asked us to concentrate.

"We must will the force to circle through the table," she said.

Which way, I wondered? What if I willed the force clockwise and everyone else willed it in the opposite direction? Would failure be my fault and my future undoing?

"Feel the force going around the table," she said. "Let it flow with your energy."

In a few minutes, and to my surprise, I did feel a force traveling in a circle through and around the top of the table. I concentrated on my hands, injecting as much energy as I could into that maelstrom before me.

"Keep your hands on the table," informed Mrs. Stout, who, with furrowed brow and concentrated vision, displayed a pose of total absorption while her children exhibited signs of equal engagement. As for myself, I did my best and hoped I was not a distraction.

"Now move your palms back until they are off the table, or the force will become too strong for us tonight."

Each of us followed her directions until only our fingers remained on the table.

"Is anyone there?" asked Mrs. Stout.

The energy disrupted into fits of stops and starts, like choppy water caused by intersecting ocean currents. The table moved slightly upwards and then dropped to the floor, either released by the force that had raised it up from above or pulled it down by a force from below. I did not know which.

"If you are there, answer 'yes' with one knock and 'no' with two."

The corner of the table between the two children moved slightly off the floor and returned.

"Is that a yes," asked Mrs. Stout.

The leg rose up and quickly returned to the floor one time.

"Do we know you?"

Two knocks. No.

"Are you a man?"

One knock. Yes.

"Are you an early settler?"

Two knocks. No

"Earlier?"

One knock. Yes.

"Are you an Indian?"

One knock. Yes.

"Were you an Iroquois?"

Two knocks. No

"Were you here before the others?"

One knock. Yes

This went on for a while and I lost track of time.

Mrs. Stout said the Indian might be a member of the Adena culture that built the burial mounds and didn't know why he was still here. That anyone was around after they died, available to communicate with the living, or had any desire to do so, was a complete surprise to me, if indeed, it was happening at all.

"I'd like to know where he is from," she said, "but I can't ask about landmarks that don't exist anymore." Her focus returned to the table. "Is your resting place nearby?"

One knock. Yes.

"Near the river?"

One knock. Yes.

We continued for another ten minutes with no conclusion as to why he communicated with us, what he wanted, or what we could do for him. A final resting place nearby could be anywhere as the Indians traveled on the Monongahela that meandered north until it connected with the Ohio.

How Mrs. Stout contacted someone so ancient, I'll never know. If she and her children fabricated the table tipping, I will never know that, either. I detected no gaming or deceit on anyone's part. The living room lights had not been dimmed, and I did feel a force of energy swirling around the table beneath my hands, but of course, our brains are adaptable enough to allow us to believe anything we wish. I can tell you this, however, that wasn't the only time we communicated with the deceased in the Stouts' continuously changing antique-furnished living room.

The next afternoon, I came back to the house early and found Annie on the phone with her father. Mrs. Stout was in bed with one of her migraine headaches, and Annie asked if he could come home early to take care of her. I didn't want to eavesdrop, but I got the impression that he couldn't or wouldn't.

"Whenever Mom uses the table," Annie said to me, "she has to stay in bed the next day to get better."

I guessed that would have been one of the reasons Mr. Stout did not participate. He might not have believed, or he might have believed, but either way, he saw the damage that comes from doing the conceivably impossible with no recognizable benefit. His belief in that respect was not uncommon. Many West Virginians I met were basic, insightful people. They cared less about what you did, and more about the difference you made in doing it. If you didn't make a difference, you were wasting your time.

Annie went on to tell me, as if in confession, that her father was the only soldier in his company to survive the war, and that him knowing this was often more than he could tolerate in a day. She said he went to church every Sunday to pray for their souls and that her mother was his only support when she was capable. And then, following a long pause, she said, "When he's in the basement, I think he talks to those men."

Relieved of her burden, Annie offered a little smile, then retreated to her room.

Weeks went by. I continued with my college classes, Mr. Stout continued working on projects in the basement, and Mrs. Stout continued selling her living room furniture and filling the empty spaces with what remained in the garage on the other side of the path. I don't remember her ever buying more furniture, and wondered when she would run out. I began looking at the furniture as an inheritance to be sold off in hard times.

One rainy evening, Mr. and Mrs. Stout were out, and young Willie was sick in bed with a mild fever. Annie and I were in his room to keep him company. She asked if I would like to try the table. I thought it would be fun, but I did not believe the two of us would be able to make it work.

We sat with the card table between us in Willie's bedroom ten feet away, with our palms down and all the concentration we could muster. To my surprise, the table began to move. As the energy grew, we moved our palms off the table, then testing the limits of our power, we held on with only four fingers, then three and then only two. The table continued to rock back and forth on its legs.

"Go find Willie," said Annie. With no more than two fingers on either side, the table danced across the room to Willie's bedside.

I remember, in this case, being exhilarated, even euphoric over the entire event. I felt that I had been let in on a secret and allowed to tap into a power that would change my life. But while I sat immersed in my new-found state, there was little reaction from either of the children, which led me to guess that this activity and the energy it generated were common occurrences and made little difference in their lives.

One morning, a short while later, Mr. Stout told me to leave the house. I asked him why.

"You know why," he said.

I didn't, but at my young age, didn't press the matter. for fear of uncovering an unforgivable sin I had blocked from my memory.

I found a room in a walkout basement, not far away, and moved in that afternoon. Rooms were easy to come by, as everyone was renting what they had to college students. The owner, a cheerful man, worked for an undertaker and mentioned that he was required to leave at all hours of the day and night to pick up bodies anywhere within a thirty-mile radius. He said I could come along if I liked. He would welcome the company and the extra help.

Three months later, on a Thursday afternoon, my landlord asked if I would like to go with him to pick up someone who had just passed away. This would be my first, and, although feeling squeamish, I said yes. We drove to the funeral parlor to pick up the hearse and an assistant then drove back to my previous address.

Mr. Stout, Annie and Willie were sitting in the living room on, what I later learned from Annie, was their last antique couch, which they had to sell to pay for the funeral. We walked upstairs and brought Mrs. Stout down on a gurney wrapped in a sheet.

We would bring her to the funeral home where the funeral director would preserve her features. The hearse would deliver her to church, and when the service came to an end, the hearse would take her to the cemetery for burial. When that happened, I hoped she would get to meet and learn more about that Indian.

On my way out the front door that afternoon, I couldn't look at the family for fear of what they were thinking or what they might say. Mr. Stout had told me to leave his house and never return, and now I was back helping carry his wife out the front door and out of his life. With my hands on the gurney, I felt that I was removing what was left of his resources and leaving him alone in the basement of his home with the ghosts of those soldiers in his last foxhole.

North Carolina 2003

Self-Improvement

It was only 9:30 an' already hot outside, and the short walk from my trailer to hers started me to wilting. Janet was my neighbor and, I guess, my best friend. I didn't really have no one else. I'd been dating my husband Jake since the ninth grade an' he took care of me until he went to Fort Bragg to join the Army and we had a baby girl before I graduated.

"Come on in and sit down you poor thing. How's that little girl of yours? Ina's such a beautiful name."

It was gonna be another hot day, and the air conditioner in our trailer didn't work that good, and I just couldn't un-stick the back of my dress from any part of my body.

"You drop Ina off at the day care like I told you? It's a real nice place for that little girl to play with other children. And you'll get to meet some of the mothers here on the base."

Janet reached over an' touched my arm. "You know, Mary Lou, around here you just got to have someone to talk to, or you'll end up in Section 8. An' I hear they got a special ward set up somewhere just for us wives."

Janet had two boys in school, and her husband was a sergeant in another unit. They had already done one tour and got to live in Germany. They sure were lucky. Maybe Jake would get a tour like that an' we could live in a nice place somewhere, except Jake didn't have that much good luck. He'd been in for two years and hadn't made rank. I know he's got a temper, but there's some unit leader who don't like him, an' Jake told me he's got to transfer out to get a fair shake.

Sometimes I took a train back home to spend time with my momma to give Jake time to be alone when he's had hard duty. Once he slept through revelry and got extra duty for a week, which I don't understand 'cause if they work you so hard why don't they let you get the rest you need?

"I'm getting us some coffee," said Janet "An' Mary Lou, we're real proud of you taking those school courses so you could get your diploma. I bet you never knew you were so smart."

I had to admit Janet was right. My brain just naturally remembers stuff and it wasn't that hard. I'd remember a lot more if I had the time.

"Have you thought anymore about going to school to learn a job liked we talked about? I bet you'd be a real good nurse."

That was Janet's idea. I'd never think to be a nurse. I don't know who I could take care of, except my Ina. If it was anyone else, I wouldn't know what I'd do.

"You remember when my boy got hurt, an' we took him to the dispensary? They took blood from his arm and give him a Tetanus shot and you held his arm and didn't mind one bit. Most people can't stand the sight of blood and it don't bother you at all."

I didn't know why blood don't bother me, but I could never go to school to be a nurse. When would I ever have the time, taking care of Ina, an' the good Lord knows, Jake don't make enough money for me to go to school. He wouldn't stand for it anyway.

"Here's your coffee? Now Mary Lou, I wish I had a mirror. Look at yourself all scrunched over like a sack of hay on a hot day, which it is today, I will admit."

I looked down at my coffee just staring into its darkness.

"Why, you're holding up your head with one hand an' trying to drink your coffee with the other which nobody can do unless you're one of those contortionists you see at the carnival. The only thing I can see is that curly brown hair of yours."

I raised my eyes up and looked at Janet. She was right. She was always right. I just grew up with my head down, doing what I was told, never thinking about anything.

"Mary Lou?"

I sat up in my chair tall and straight and put both hands in my lap and looked right at Janet.

She laughed. "That's better, but how you supposed to pick up that coffee with both hands in your lap?"

So, I picked up the coffee with my right hand, which was hard until I put the other hand on the table to balance myself, and then I lifted that cup right up off the table and took a drink, sitting up with my shoulders back and my eyes straight ahead. Janet looked at me an' gave me a big smile while she adjusted her own self as well.

"Well, you are a pretty little thing, Miss Mary Lou, an' you're smart too. All you got to remember is to look ahead. Don't you never mind the past."

Sometimes when I was with Janet, I thought she was right, that I could do anything. But most of the time I can only think about what Jake would do if he found out. He always said he liked me the way I was and didn't want me to change or do anything different. He said nothing should ever come between him and me. I knew he hit me sometimes, but it wasn't his fault. If things were better for him he'd be a lot happier. I didn't know if Janet knew about that. I never told her, and she never said nothing.

"When we were down in Georgia, and my if you think it's hot here, whew, I had a friend who was pretty and smart just like you," said Janet.

She always said things that made me feel good.

"When my friend told me about her life, I just knew we had to do something an' that she was due some self-improvement. Her husband was in the 42nd and was away a lot, an' when he was home he wasn't very nice. Would you like to know what she did?"

At first, I wasn't sure how someone else's life could be like mine an' didn't see how anything this woman did mattered to me, but I guessed it wouldn't hurt to listen, so I nodded yes.

"My friend said how she felt trapped and had no place to go and no money, and just had more problems than you could shake a stick at. She didn't even have family to help her. Well, we figured out a couple of things she might have done if she had never met her husband, and one was she wanted to be a teacher. So, we looked at where she could go to school to become a teacher and then went an' talked to those people even though she was still trapped with no money and no time. What she found out was feeling trapped was a powerful state of mind, but that's all it is, cause once you decide what you want to do, figuring out how to get there isn't that hard if you have a plan."

And that's how Janet got me thinking about being a nurse and where I could go to school an' that the most important thing was to talk to people who believed in me and not to talk to anyone who didn't. If that meant keeping some secrets from Jake, I guessed that was okay as long as he didn't find out.

Just believing in something made me a stronger person 'cause Janet said lots of people make excuses for not doing anything, but I wasn't one of those people. When we talked in those hot sticky days I felt like I was getting my life back even if it was only with Janet and her husband, the sergeant. It was her husband who said I should spend a few minutes each day doing some physical exercise to stay in shape and he took me an showed me just what to do. He said that if I got stronger, it wouldn't hurt so much if someone hit me. That was the first time I really talked to anyone about that, but I would never say anything about Jake threatening me with his gun.

One day I came over to Janet's after Jake hit me. She held me close for the longest time while I had a few tears and then she sat me down.

"Well, Mary Lou, I just don't know what it feels like to be hit by someone, 'cause it never happened to me. I never had a boyfriend who hit me, and my husband doesn't hit me, and I don't have any friends who get hit by their husbands, except you. What's it like, Mary Lou?"

Now I really began to cry because I was ashamed to talk about it, not because I couldn't, but because I didn't want anyone to think my marriage was any different than theirs, an' I didn't want anyone to think my marriage wasn't getting better or that my husband was a bad person or that I was a bad person.

"Mary Lou. Do you have any friends whose husbands hit them? Do you even know anyone who gets hit by their husband?

Janet wasn't making me feel any better 'because I didn't know anyone. I was the only one. When I first got hit, I thought it must happen to lots of people, an' I heard it does, but I didn't know anyone. Then Janet pulled me up off the chair and took my wrist and held my hand up in the air.

"Show me how he hits you. Go ahead. Show me."

I placed my arm across my chest and slowly swung my arm up toward Janet's face to show her what Jake does. I was showing her the worst secret of my life. She held up her arm in front of herself when I did it. She asked me to do it again and each time I only hit at her arm never coming close to her face.

"Mary Lou, would you hit your daughter like that?"

I frowned at her and thought that was an awful thing to say.

"Of course, you wouldn't. No one would, that I know of. Then, what kind of man would do that to his wife?"

Another morning, her husband the sergeant, came home and talked about how no man had the right to hit a woman and how women had the right to protect themselves. He said he knew my husband an' said I should protect myself from him. He said to watch how Janet would protect herself from Jake. He turned a little and swung the back of his hand at Janet so fast I didn't see it until she screamed and was hit and fell backwards to the couch and began to cry. I jumped back scared to death. I wanted to run, but Janet was crying. Her husband just walked off into the kitchen. Then Janet got up and asked if I wanted a cup of coffee. I didn't understand. Then her husband said the coffee was ready. Janet walked over to her husband and smiled.

"I didn't get hurt, Mary Lou."

She came over to me and took my hand and walked me to the table where we both sat down. She said she pretended everything when she was hit, and that I could learn to protect myself the same way if I would hold up my hands, step back and bend a little. They said they'd teach me, right after we finished our coffee.

They both held onto me and showed me what to do and we practiced for a while until I had to go. Janet told me that this was one way to protect myself when bad things were happening and that I had to learn to always be in control to protect the baby. I have to admit it worked out well especially when Jake had been drinking.

One day I was at Janet's when she introduced me to a friend who sold life insurance. He explained the importance of protecting my daughter, Ina, in case anything ever happened to Jake or me and that a small policy was easy to get, and you wouldn't have to pay any premiums for the first year. I knew Jake probably wouldn't agree but Janet said I could sign his name, and they'd hold on to the policy so

Jake wouldn't find out and get angry, then our baby girl would be protected. After me and Janet signed all the insurance papers, I felt a lot better for my Ina.

October came, and the weather was finally cooling off. I dropped Ina off at day care, an' Janet said she wanted to have some fun and we were going for a ride. We drove through the base to a big building I had seen only once before. We showed our ID cards and wrote our name in a book and walked down the hallway, then pushed open a door to the outside where we stood in a booth. Janet opened a bag and took out a small gun that I thought was really pretty. She put in some bullets and shot at a target. She hit the red bull's eye every time. She put some more bullets in the gun and showed me how to aim. It was a pretty silver gun with a pink handle, and I loved to hold it. The gun made a lot of noise at first, but after a few weeks of shooting, it didn't bother me at all. Janet said she had a friend who had a gun just like hers and wanted to sell it and was in no hurry for the money. So, I got my permit, and Janet gave me the gun. We practiced at the range every chance we got.

Just before Christmas, Jake didn't get promoted again, and got so mad he hit me, though it didn't hurt that much thanks to Janet, but now he was hitting me in front of Ina and threatening me with his gun. Janet said I should visit Momma to give Jake some rest and that's what I did.

While I was back home, Momma looked after Ina, and I got to talk to the people at the college and learned about their nursing program. They were real nice and showed me around the campus and the rooms and laboratories where I'd be taking classes. I could finish in three years and get a job, and then go back and take some extra courses for a bachelor's degree if I wanted. I told them I didn't know when I would be able to start because, right now, I was at Fort Bragg with my husband. They asked me how I liked the Army, and I said it was all right. I wasn't going to tell them anything about Jake. They said I should go downtown and talk to a recruiter about what I wanted to do, and they could probably help. They gave me some pamphlets and forms, so I could apply to their program. When I left, the sun was shining.

The next day I walked to the Army recruiter and told him I was thinking about going to the college for nursing and wanted to know what programs they had. The recruiter was a man and said they had a great program for people like me. He asked if I could come back tomorrow when a female recruiter would be there, because she knew a lot more than he did. I said okay and returned the next day.

The woman recruiter was real nice and said that if I got my degree in nursing and joined the Army, they would pay for any more schooling I wanted, and I'd be a junior officer with officer pay. I was shocked as all get out. I would be an officer. Oh God, Jake would have a fit if I was to become an officer, and he didn't have rank. But then I began to laugh, 'cause that was really funny.

Two weeks later I took a train back to the base and saw Jake when he came home around supper. He was surprised to see me, but that's all I could tell. He told me he was leaving next week to go to Florida fishing with some of his buddies. I didn't even know he liked fishing, but I guess he just wanted to get away. When I told Janet, she said that before he left, I should tell him my plans, so he'd have time to think about it before he came back. I was surprised she said that, but she always knows what's best. She told me her husband knew the men he was going with, an' they weren't really Jake's buddies, but he was just going along. She said that if there were any trouble her husband would hear about it and let her know.

The next weekend Jake packed his things and got ready for his bus to Florida. He said he'd rent the equipment he needed. Just before he walked out the door, I did what Janet said and told him about my idea to go to college to become a nurse and maybe become an officer at the Army hospital. He looked at me like he didn't hear, and then he went crazy yelling that I was too stupid to become a nurse, and the Army wouldn't want anything to do with me. He hit me and knocked me down into the couch and took out his gun and threatened me to get those ideas out of my head.

Two days letter I got a call in the afternoon from Janet who said that Jake was having problems in Florida, and I should take the train down there right away. Her husband, the sergeant, was already there and would help me, and while I was gone she would take care of Ina.

The train pulled into Gainesville late at night, and Janet's husband showed me to a room where I could freshen up, then he took me to a bar where I could find Jake. When we got there, it was almost eleven. Jake was sitting at a table talking pretty loud, bragging about something I didn't understand.

I walked over and stood behind the man sitting across from Jake. At first, I don't think he saw me. Then he looked at me kind of funny and stood up knocking his chair over. He yelled at me saying what was I doing in Florida. He had no right to speak to me that way and I asked him back where'd he get the money to be carrying on like this when we barcly had enough to eat and what about our daughter, Ina. He pointed his finger at me and started swearing about what was I doing here, and why wasn't I home taking care of the baby, which is what he said because he didn't even know Ina was growing up and almost four years old.

Jake came around the table at me, so I backed away and continued walking backwards right out the door with him yelling at me. When he was outside, he told me he had his gun with him, and I deserved to be shot for ruining his life. I moved away as far as I could go and had my back up against one of the parked cars. I was holding my purse with my left hand, and my right hand was inside holding my gun like Janet showed me. Jake reached under his shirt, and I didn't look on after that.

I was never so scared in my life, but I did what Janet told me and pulled the trigger three times, which is what Janet said I should do. She told me if you were serious, pull the trigger three times an' if you weren't serious, you shouldn't have a gun in the first place. Jake fell to the ground, and in no time, the police were there. They took my gun and had me sit in the back of a police car away from everybody.

A police officer in regular clothes came over and asked me what happened, and then went an' talked to the sergeant and the other men. I can't say I felt sorry for Jake because I was protecting myself an' Ina from being without a mother. The officer returned and told me that everyone agreed I had acted in self- defense, and under Florida Law I was free to go. He even handed me my gun and told me to keep it for protection. Janet's husband came over and took me to the station. He got me on a train and said I should get some sleep and not worry about what happened.

The next day at the base I had a long talk with Janet, and she said I should follow my plan to go back home to live with my mother while I went to school to become a nurse and that the insurance policy would pay for it.

I signed up for classes and knew in three years I would be a nurse and maybe even an officer in the Army. Just before my tuition was due, I received a check from Janet for $250,000, that she said came from the insurance policy. I was never so shocked in my life to see such money. This was more than I had ever seen and much more than I needed to live on and go to school, so the first thing I did was buy a real nice car and pay Momma's bills.

After I was settled in school, I wrote a letter to Janet and her husband.

"Look what came in the mail today."

"What?"

"A nice letter from Mary Lou, thanking us for talking her into getting that insurance policy. She says the quarter million is enough to pay her tuition and start a savings account for her daughter.

"Good for her," said the sergeant.

"Have you paid your buddies for bringing Jake down to Florida?"

"Yes, I did. Did you ever get around to telling Mary Lou there were two policies on Jake for a quarter million each?"

Janet smiled at their standard joke. "Never had a chance, but I met the wife of that recruit you told me about. That poor thing could sure use our help."

The Deer Stand

Jacque Franale lay beneath the deer stand with his left leg broken and crushed just above the ankle by his own bear trap, staked to the ground under a six-inch covering of snow. In less than an hour, he would bleed to death, but the extreme pain and shock to his body from this gruesome accident would render him unconscious well before that time. The throbbing agony he felt was unimaginable, and his guttural moans pierced the silence of the north woods' pristine solitude.

Tom Stark had witnessed the grisly scene and offered Franale a chance to end his pain and atone for his sins. He handed Franale the deer rifle with one bullet in the chamber and walked away. Stark climbed up the snow-covered outcropping of granite where he could look down twenty feet into a ravine filled with brush and small pine. In better times he would sit there in silence, watching baby deer follow their mother through the pass to a lair he never found.

Franale held the rifle to his body and pulled the trigger. The rasping sound of deep pain ended. Only the whisper of a cold breeze could be heard making its way through the pine. Snow began to fall and would continue for the next three days covering the intemperate past until spring.

Tom Stark had left his home the day after Thanksgiving for the cabin in Coos County he inherited from his grandfather. Spending time there between Thanksgiving and Christmas was an opportunity to live simply and find peace before the holiday season, which had always brought stress and disappointment.

Light snow fell in New Jersey but did not stick, while a foot of snow covered the northern woods of New Hampshire, snow that would not melt until late spring. He would leave the snowmobile home until January when the local clubs had packed down and mark the trails.

The cabin was a twenty by twenty-four log-structure built with timber that had been cut from the land. His grandfather built a stone flu for the wood stove at one end and two sets of bunk beds at the other. There were two four-foot-long shelves of wide plank board braced to the wall used to store food and supplies above the kitchen counter, a soapstone sink and hand pump. A hand pump inside the cabin had been a luxury sixty years ago and remains a convenience to this day. The front door was centered on the south side protected by a porch roof the length of the cabin. A portable kerosene heater provided comfort in the spring and fall and a minimal warmth in the winter until a fire in the wood stove threw enough heat to overcome the coldest weather.

After bringing the temperature up to above freezing with the kerosene heater, Stark built a fire in the wood stove to warm the cabin for the night. Next morning, he shoveled a forty-five-yard path through the snow to the wood stacked between two trees, ten feet beyond an old deer stand that had not been used since his grandfather passed away. In three trips, he carried the day's supply back to the cabin, stacking the two-foot lengths on the porch next to the front door. At noon, he placed another log inside the firebox, closed the door, and reduced the airflow to its lowest level.

Stark drove to Henry's General Store for supplies, loaded them onto the back seat of his truck, then walked next door to the Riverside Diner for lunch. Every building abutting the gravel parking lay eight feet above the Ammonoosuc River, and it was a wonder they were still standing after ninety years of annual flooding and constant abuse. This river, flowing slowly over rocks and gravel a few yards below, could be easily dismissed in the summer and winter months as a shallow stream that barely trickles over the rocks and pebbles beneath it, but after the snow melt and spring rain, the river can become a healthy force of raging water that only a fool would attempt to cross.

Before returning to the cabin, Stark spent an hour driving along the back roads to reacquaint himself with the tranquil beauty of this unspoiled landscape. Along the highway, he passed the familiar narrow farmhouse with an attached barn, and a mile later, the white cabins built along a riverbed that were now closed for the winter. He felt at home. Two miles further, he passed a small restaurant and lounge he would visit later that evening.

Stark drove the familiar loop until he returned to the narrow road that bordered his property before it continued over the state line into Vermont. He pulled into the dirt driveway between two maples and carried his supplies inside. The wood stove was still warm, and when he opened the vent, the glowing embers returned to full blaze, heating the cabin to sixty-five degrees. The routine of living here for short periods during the winter months was coming back, and he felt at ease with the slower pace.

After storing the supplies, Stark attached snowshoes to his boots and began the one-mile survey of his property line. An hour on, he came to a wide stream that had not yet frozen, and having no access to the other side, moved north along the edge until he reached the state forest boundary, then turned southward to his cabin.

Half of the land he owned was a wooded hill that led upwards for a quarter mile until it became a private forest owned by the paper mills. Northeast from the woodpile the land dropped into a ravine that offered protection for deer, moose, woodcocks, and anything else that needed shelter. He was pleased with the land and did not look forward to returning home the following week.

Stark entered the restaurant later than he planned and had his choice of several empty booths. He took the one furthest from the front door for protection from the cold that crawled over the threshold and along the floor. A family of three occupied a second booth, and an older couple sat in a third. Any other customers they had served that evening had either left or moved to the bar through a double door next to the kitchen entrance. The waitress brought the bill to the family of three, asked the older couple if they would like some dessert then walked over to Stark and took his order for a roast beef dinner. She brought it out ten minutes later.

"That was fast," he said.

"The kitchen's getting ready to close an' the cook wants to go home."

Stark looked past the waitress to the front door and saw that a closed sign had been placed in the window.

"Glad I didn't miss it then."

She smiled. "Me too." After a slight pause, she added, "We don't want anyone to go hungry."

"What happens after nine?"

"Not much. Bar's open to eleven."

Stark finished eating paid the bill plus tip and walked into the lounge. He ordered a beer and sat down at a small table where he could watch the room. Three men were drinking off to his left, and two more were playing pool in a separate room with a cue rack on the wall and a low-hanging light over the table. The players, who looked like high school kids, left twenty minutes later, and shortly after that, the woman who had waited on him sat at the bar and asked for a glass of wine. She talked to the bartender for a few minutes, turned and made eye contact with Stark, and invited herself over.

"Slow night," he said as she sat down.

"Where you from?"

"New Jersey. Got a cabin a few miles up from here."

"How long you staying?"

"Few days. Getting ready for snowmobiling in January."

"Lot of that up here."

They talked until eleven as if they had known each other in the past and were compelled to catch up in the short time remaining before the doors were locked for the night. The bar closed, and they walked outside. The air was cold and penetrating, encouraging them not to linger.

"I'm off tomorrow night, why don't you come over for supper?"

"Are you sure?"

"I don't see why not," she said. "It's just a meal."

She drove off while Stark thought about the invitation. Backing out, he noticed there were only two other vehicles in the lot. The one of most interest was an oversized pickup with double rear wheels and an aluminum tailpipe running up the side of the cab. 'Heavy hauling,' he thought.

Inside the bar, one of the men had paid attention to the amount of time the waitress spent talking to the stranger. His name was Franale. He was not a tall man, but he was broad-shouldered with arms and hands as strong as any man who had wielded an axe most of his life and made a living hauling and lifting anything that needed to be moved.

Franale put his money on the table and walked to his truck. He waited for Stark's car to disappear around the first curve before pulling out. He had little control over his emotions and more than once had come close to spending a night in jail. Franale kept his distance, and when Stark turned left onto his road, realized this was the out-of-state guy with the cabin he had heard about.

He continued to an abandoned logging road, removed the chain and drove in. Though a foot of snow covered the ground, the truck had no trouble powering through in low gear. Twenty minutes later, he stopped, grabbed his deer rifle from the rear window gun rack and jogged a quarter mile through the woods until he saw light coming from the cabin windows. When Franale reached the wood pile, he stopped to catch his breath. His anger turned to frustration when he realized he didn't know what he wanted to do. *I'll give him a warning*, he thought.

Franale circled around to the front of the cabin, raised his rifle, and fired. The bullet lodged into the first inch of the two-inch thick cross-layered oak door, stopping at a metal brace, and though the sound of the rifle was startling, the bullet did little damage. Franale stood behind a row of bayberry bushes waiting for a response but heard no sound and saw no movement. Angered, he retraced his steps toward the woodpile, stopped at the deer stand, and fired two rounds into the footrest, splintering the frame.

The next morning, Stark followed the footprints past the woodpile to the logging road where Franale had parked his truck. The double rear wheel tires left an unmistakable signature in the snow.

That evening, on his way to the waitress's house, Stark slowed down as he approached the restaurant. He spotted the large truck parked in the lot and drove close enough to read the license plate.

"I brought a bottle of Henry's best red," said Stark.

"Thanks," said the waitress. "I'll get it breathing. The glasses are by the sink."

The young woman had roasted a chicken and vegetables in the oven and boiled rice on the stove.

"Would you mind if I asked about the people in the bar last night?"

"Just the regulars," she said.

"Who owns the pickup with a double set of rear wheels?"

She sat down at the table. "Why?"

"I don't think he likes me." Stark didn't see any reason to tell her his cabin had been used for target practice.

"Jacque Franale. He lives in a farmhouse a mile after you pass the restaurant. Been there his whole life."

Stark took his first sip of wine. "What does he do?"

"Hunts, traps. Food stamps since he got fired."

"From what?"

"Used to work at the bar until he started arguing with customers. He's short on temper and long on opinion, like a lot of folks around here."

Their conversation delayed the meal until late. After a brief hug, Tom buttoned his jacket and drove back to the cabin.

Two minutes after Stark left, the waitress heard a knock on the door. When she opened it, Jacque Franale pushed his way inside. Though they had been divorced for over a year, he was unable to control his jealousy. He slapped her across the face and pushed her back into the kitchen. He grabbed her left arm, but she pulled free. She had suffered through his anger before, which was why the restraining order was still in place. She backed against the counter, grabbed a kitchen knife and swung wide.

Franale raised his left arm to protect his face and the blade sliced through his shirt and the first two layers of his skin. Blood welled up and began dripping down onto the floor. He grabbed his arm to stop the bleeding only to watch the dark fluid ooze through his tightly clenched fist.

She pointed the knife at his chest. "Get out! Or when the cops come, they'll find your body on the floor."

She threw him a dirty dish towel. "Wrap it up and get the hell out!"

Next evening Stark returned to the restaurant for dinner. Franale was at the bar favoring his left arm, and the waitress was wearing makeup. After eating, he told the waitress he had an errand to run but would be back for a drink before closing.

Stark drove to the farmhouse and parked his car in the driveway. The house was off limits, but the barn looked like it had never been closed, leaving the contents open to inspection. The rundown building was stacked with hundreds of discarded items of every description. Stark pulled out a flashlight and walked inside. Muskrat and beaver traps hung on nails pounded into the wall. Further back, next to a storage box, he found a large trap with a serial number stamped into the frame. He had read about these and the reasons they had been outlawed, but it was the first time he had ever seen the powerful jaws of a bear trap. He took it with him and drove back to his cabin. From the small shed, he grabbed a wooden stake, hammer, and a rake, then walked to the deer stand, cleared an area of snow, set the trap and staked the chain into the ground. He covered the trap with snow, and walking backwards, raked the path until he reached the cabin.

An hour later Stark was sitting at a table inside the bar waiting for the waitress to get off duty. When she joined him, he ordered a glass of wine. She smiled appreciatively but remained silent.

"You had a visitor last night."

"Forget it."

"No one around here's taking notice."

"He was my husband until a year ago. It was a bad match. I guess I didn't know him as well as I thought."

"If we knew everything there was to know about someone, we'd probably never get married."

They talked until closing and walked out the door. Stark suggested that his cabin might be safer than her apartment. The cabin had bunk beds, so she would be safe from him as well.

"All right," she said. "Follow my car so I can get some things."

She drove behind her apartment house to stay out of sight then went up the outside stairs, put together a small bag, and returned to his truck. When they reached the cabin, he backed into a low shed, covered it with an old tarpaulin, and stacked some wood in front to hide its appearance. Stark raked out that tire tracks and footprints right up to the cabin. Once they were inside, he used the kerosene heater so there would be no wood smoke in the air.

Next morning Stark woke to a chilly cabin and gray skies but was pleased they had slept through the night undisturbed. He looked out and saw no sign of Franale. Stark opened the wood stove, put some rolled-up newspaper on top of the ashes, filled it with kindling, and lit the paper. Once the kindling had caught, he placed two logs in the firebox and kept the door open until they burst into flame.

The waitress was now up and stood in the kitchen appreciating the heat from the wood stove. "Good morning," she said.

"Morning," said Stark. "I'm going out for more wood. I'll be right back."

He made his way through the snow, picked up an armload of logs, brought them to the porch then returned for another load.

The waitress turned around to pump water for a pot of coffee. A bullet shattered the cabin window and hit the waitress just below her shoulder blade, exploding her heart, and continuing until it lodged into the cabin wall.

At the sound of the rifle, Stark ducked behind the woodpile and waited.

"Se Lever! Se Lever! You stand up, you might live!"

Franale walked slowly through the woods toward the woodpile, hunched down with one finger on the trigger. He reached the deer stand and stepped into the bear trap that slammed shut above his ankle, cutting into his leg and crushing his bones. The harsh blow took his breath away. The sudden impact and excruciating pain caused him to drop the rifle and scream in agony, gasping for air between spasms.

Stark stood up and ran to the cabin suspecting the worse. He opened the door to find the waitress lying on the blood-stained cabin floor. Catching his breath, he jogged back to the deer stand, picked up Franale's rifle and raised it to his head. "You son-of-a-bitch!"

He wanted the satisfaction of pulling the trigger until he realized Franale suffering a slow death was a more fitting end, and then he had a better idea.

"You're a dead man," he yelled at Franale. "Your gonna' bleed out right here, so look around, because this is the last thing you'll ever see."

He removed the shells from the rifle, placed one to the chamber and handed him the gun with the muzzle pointed at his neck.

"If you want to stop the pain, you'll have to do it yourself."

Franale held the barrel in place with his left hand and lowered his right to the trigger.

Stark turned and walked to the ledge where he could look down to the tops of the snow-covered pine. He waited less than a minute before the guttural sounds of Franale's agony ended with a single 30-30 bullet cutting through flesh and bone.

*

By early spring, when the waters took possession of the riverbanks, the owner of Henry's store had seen no activity in the direction of Stark's cabin since the holidays and mentioned it to the warden who said he would go up and take a look.

The next afternoon, state police found the deteriorated corpse of Franale's ex-wife four months dead from a bullet that shattered her internal organs. Thirty-five yards away beneath a splintered deer stand, they found the grisly sight of a dead man with his foot nearly severed by an illegal bear trap registered to Franale. The deer rifle by his side was the one used to kill the woman in the cabin.

The police report concluded that: the victim in the bear trap, identified as Jacque Franale, had placed said trap on the property of Tom Stark as part of the harassment Stark reported to the police last fall, that Franale killed his ex-wife by shooting her in the back with his rifle, and that Jacque Franale walked back to the deer stand on the way to his truck when he accidentally stepped into his own bear trap and died.

*

The following November, a hunter, tracking a six-point buck through the ravine, discovered human remains, which were later identified as Tom Stark. A forensic team determined that Stark had been shot in the back with a 30-30 deer rifle and most likely died instantly.

The warden was never able to determine whether Stark was shot before Franale killed his ex-wife or after, but he did know that two men and one woman in the north woods was a poor mix no matter how you planned your day.

Rhode Island 1979

The Boss's Wife

D aniel posted the following message. *Gone to the other side. Thanks for all the fun. Hope we can still be friends. Expect no mercy.*

That evening he bought the first round of beer for his friends as a gesture of good will while explaining his decision to move on. Everyone else would have to wait until they logged on to his website.

Two years earlier, Daniel had started a small computer consulting business while looking for a job that didn't exist. He relaxed by engaging in the one skill he had mastered during four years of learning to write software code which was hacking into customer accounts at financial institutions. The data he uncovered served to highlight his meager earnings compared to the income of those who took thousands in advances, bonuses, and fees. First, he was surprised and then he became angry. These people piled up their wealth through duplicity and deceit, no brainpower required, only greed and guile. He decided to employ his skills for his own financial gain.

To test the waters, Daniel hacked into local banks, with firewalls that were easy to penetrate. He transferred money in and out of accounts and waited for a response from either the banks or the feds. None came, and amazingly, the accounts did not change, making him realize that most people with a lot of money seldom check their balances. As his proficiency increased, he moved to targets with higher levels of security. He established an account in a New York bank as the first receiver of funds, from which he later transferred money to an offshore account. The New York bank was selected because he discovered the Mafia used it to launder money. The first name on the account he created was Anthony, one of the most common first names in the phone book and the last name on the account was Genovese, one of the most feared names in all of New York.

Daniel and his friends sharpened their skills by hacking into encrypted data several times a week, the same way musicians sharpen their skills by practicing their instruments on an equally vigorous schedule. For fun, they competed in a scramble. Each member would hack into the same target on successive nights, retrieve data, and compare their access times.

It was during one of these competitions, that Daniel received an unnerving message on his screen that read: *i admire your wor.*

He typed back: *who are you*

The reply was an internet address. He jotted it down, closed his laptop, and walked out of the coffee shop.

Daniel's first step was to rule out a friend playing a joke. In a shared email account, he typed a short note to the editor of a local newspaper then moved it to a draft folder. The group would access the draft and read his request for a meeting. The name of the newspaper was code for a designated restaurant. Standard time was 7:30 pm.

Daniel got there before the others and selected a rear booth where he could watch the door.

Anthony was next to arrive. His rugged six-foot build, with suit, shined black shoes and short hair, screamed cop, an appearance he embraced because that's what he was. He was the voice of reason relied on in times of trouble.

Anthony had developed computer software that would plot the date, time, type, and location of every crime in the city. Based on this information, the program would generate probable future crime sites.

The crime rate went down, and his boss was happy. He also paid attention to organized crime by hacking into their accounts to track the flow of laundered money but kept these activities to himself. For fun, he also tracked where the syndicate spent their leisure time. He even knew where their wives went shopping. No one would have suspected Anthony of trolling through secure networks reading the percent of gross skimmed off the price of expensive dresses stored on racks in the garment district, which was how he and Daniel met.

Tom and Henry arrived next. They were bright and enthusiastic, but not ready to move up the corporate ladder. Both had completed a two-year technical school, and both were employed by the same non-profit agency to run the IT department. They spent most of the day resetting passwords for staff that used their computers to display pictures of babies, pets, and boyfriends. Their prospects for earning a respectable living were less than a blacksmith's in Detroit and was a frequent topic of conversation.

"Where's Elvira?" they asked, looking to brighten up the end of another monotonous eight-hour shift reconstructing ones and zeros on an outdated network.

"Haven't seen her," said Daniel. "I have a question for you, though. Did either of you send me a message last night?"

No one at the table had, but they agreed to ask around.

"Are you being tracked? How old is your computer?" asked Anthony.

"Yes, to the first and about three months to the second." Daniel's practice was to use a cheap laptop and someone else's Wi-Fi for hacking. He operated his legitimate consulting business from desktops at home. If the FBI ever took them, there would be nothing to find.

"What did the message say?"

"I admire your work and gave me an address to reach him."

"Did you try it?"

"I didn't, in case it was a trap."

He gave Anthony the piece of paper just as the waitress came over to take their order.

Anthony looked up at her name tag. "Julie, do you have your phone with you? We're trying to settle something; can I borrow it for a moment?"

Eager to please the handsome officer, she gave Anthony her phone. He went online to the internet address and typed in: *who r u*. A minute went by with no response, so he handed the phone back with his card. "If you get a suspicious message, call me."

"The address is a message board," said Anthony.

"Someone's been screwing with me. How do you track a laptop that borrows Wi-Fi from public locations?" said Daniel.

The boys nodded, but Anthony pointed to the obvious. "Evidently they can. It means there is an algorithm out there with your name on it."

"What should I do?"

"Use a guest computer at a hotel. You won't even have to log in."

"Oh, Daniel, take me to a hotel," said Elvira, aka Dark Angel or PM for Primarily Mary, as she slid into the booth, flipped her long red hair back behind her right ear and gave everyone a warm smile. "I'll be appearing tonight as Dark Angel, if anyone is interested."

"Daniel thinks he's being watched," said Anthony.

PM smiled. "I know all about being watched, but I guess in your case, it's not a good thing." Then she frowned. "So dump your computer and lay low. If you need a place to hide, you can always lay low with me."

"Worst-case scenario," said Anthony, "the Feds have set a trap. Best case, it's another hacker who wants to meet you."

They finished eating and Anthony left the table first. His eyes swept the room for anyone paying attention to them. Seeing no one, he left. Tom and Henry moved to the bar to watch the game. Daniel was next, and PM followed.

She looked at him with a hint of sympathy. "You look beleaguered, Daniel,"

"Yes, I am beleaguered out."

"You told me no matter how good you are there's always someone better. So, you found someone. So, what?"

"It's disturbing."

"I'm not happy about some of the new girls at the club, either, but what are you gonna do." PM gave him a kiss on the cheek. "Off to work," she said.

Daniel found the hotel computer located in an alcove away from the main desk. He typed in the internet address and a message board came up. He typed: *hello.*

Two minutes later, *hello* was returned.

Daniel typed: *why do you admire my work*

because you contacted me from a hotel computer on south main

Daniel was shocked. 'Son of a b.....' he thought. He typed: *how did you track me here*

show you if you agree to meet

Daniel: *who r u*

recruiter.

who do you recruit for

highest bidder. meet me at coffee shop on park at 9:30 Friday morning.

Daniel typed in some additional information to cover his tracks. If this was a trap, he could claim he believed he was talking to a job placement website. *i run a computer consulting business, develop web sites, solve networking problems, fix jammed printers. Is that what you're looking for?*

that's exactly what we're looking for, was the reply.

He laughed to himself: 'Sure you are, and that's exactly what I was doing when you found me.'

Daniel left and drove to the club to see Dark Angel, who had just left a customer. "Can I talk to you after work?" he asked.

"Pick me up at 11:30," she said.

"Thanks." Daniel drove to his apartment fearing he'd find a team of agents turning the place upside down. To his relief, no one was there, and nothing had been touched. He took his laptop from its hiding place, erased the hard drive, removed it, wrapped it in a bar towel and smashed it with a hammer. On his way to pick up Dark Angel, he threw what remained into a scrap metal dumpster then parked by the curb next to the club entrance.

A half-hour later there was a tap on the driver's window. He looked over to see Dark Angel. As soon as she slid in, he pulled away from the curb. "Remember that message I got?"

"Your secret admirer?"

"I went to the message board, and he traced the computer I was using to the hotel. He could have been standing right behind me for all I knew."

"Awesome! What does he want?"

"Says he's recruiting for someone and wants to meet me Friday."

"So, what are you gonna do?"

Daniel didn't know and said so.

After arriving at her apartment, Dark Angel took a shower and changed. They continued talking until they were about to fall asleep. She asked him one more time. "So, what are you gonna do?"

"Guess I'll meet him Friday morning."

Anthony parked his unmarked police car across the street from the coffee shop where he could keep an eye on the building. At 9:30, Daniel took a table next to the plate-glass window where he would be visible. Two men sitting across the room finished their conversation, stood up and walked to the front door. One walked outside and the other walked over to Daniel. He could have been a college professor or a CPA. The card he handed Daniel read "Thomas Quinn, Corporate Recruiter."

"Are you the young man who fixes jammed printers?" he asked.

Daniel looked at the card. "Yes," he said.

Mr. Quinn sat down. "My client is looking for someone to work in their IT department. You'd be responsible for security only, no printers. Starting salary is $65,000. If they're satisfied with your work, your salary will increase substantially. Are you interested?"

"Why so much?"

"To keep you honest."

"How did you find me?"

"I was contacted by the person who found you nosing around his network and realized he needed more help. Does the job interest you?"

Daniel nodded yes.

"Call me tomorrow morning at the number on my card."

Two weeks later, at the age of twenty-four, Daniel began his first, full-time job. He wouldn't have to borrow money from his parents anymore, he wouldn't have to skip a meal to pay his rent, he wouldn't have to leave the country with someone else's savings, and best of all, Dark Angel moved into his apartment. All he had to do now was tell his friends that his employer was off limits. To make sure everyone understood he posted *expect no mercy* on his website.

Happiness reigned for three months then Daniel received a phone call one night telling him that Dark Angel had been kidnapped. She'd be returned unharmed if he followed a set of instructions he'd get in an hour. *This is ridiculous,* he thought. Daniel called the club only to learn that Dark Angel had not shown up for work. Reality sunk in and he sent an urgent text to Anthony, who was at his door ten minutes later.

After he explained what had happened. Anthony attached a recorder to Daniel's phone. The kidnappers called as promised and read a set of demands from a script they obviously had not written. They told Daniel to transfer two hundred and fifty-thousand dollars from the company he worked for into another account. Once he transferred the money, Dark Angel would be free to leave. They hung up before he could respond.

"What makes them think I can do that? Every key stroke we make is analyzed for consistency and blocked if it isn't. We're tighter than the CIA."

"Someone thinks you can, but not the guys reading the script. They sound like street thugs to me. I'd probably recognize their faces if I saw them."

"So now what?"

Anthony called a friend on the Organized-Crime Taskforce. He learned that the syndicate wouldn't be involved in this type of kidnapping, but he also knew that the thugs belonged to the mob. They could be Flopsy and Mopsy, but they were in the club.

"Well," said Anthony, "it's not sanctioned, so I think we'd better speak to the boss."

"Who's the boss?" asked Daniel.

"The man who runs the syndicate."

Daniel's eyes widened. "Are you kidding? They'd shoot us. Me anyway, maybe not you cause you're a cop. But definitely me."

"Not if we had his wife."

"What do you mean if we had his wife?"

"We'll put her up in a hotel room. The way I see it, his men kidnapped your girlfriend, so we'll kidnap his wife. Book a room at the Larchmont for tonight through Thursday, so it'll be available tomorrow morning."

"How're we gonna do this without getting killed?"

"They're people, just like us. Tomorrow's Wednesday. She'll be shopping alone. We'll pick her up in the parking lot."

"Without a problem?"

"If she thinks it's in her best interest, yes, without a problem. Bring your laptop."

The next morning the boss's wife stepped out of her black Lincoln just as Anthony drove up beside her. He got out and showed his badge, said there was a problem, and politely escorted her into the back seat of the police car before she could refuse. Ten minutes later, they were in the hotel room.

"Please make yourself comfortable." Anthony borrowed her cell phone to call her husband who wasn't pleased to hear a man's voice.

"Listen," said Anthony, "two of your men kidnapped a friend of mine, and I want her back, unharmed."

"We didn't kidnap nobody," said the boss, but in less polite language.

"Maybe you didn't, but the kidnappers are on your payroll." He played the recorded message over the phone. "Recognize that voice? I'll call you back in twenty minutes. And your wife's fine. Don't worry about her."

Daniel looked at the boss's wife, with fear and anguish. "The man you heard on the tape kidnapped my girlfriend," he said.

She turned away from Daniel. "Those morons."

Daniel hesitantly moved closer, afraid of what she represented. "Look, I'm sorry you're here. I really am. I only want my girlfriend back. If there's anything I can do to make it up?"

"There's nothing you can do except let me go!"

"There is something he can do for you," said Anthony. He knew her husband controlled their assets in multiple locations, doling out just enough money to keep her happy.

"I think," he said, "that you would be better protected if you had your own money in a private account that you can control in case, God forbid, something happened to your husband."

"What are you talking about?"

"Daniel can set up a personal account for you with a couple of hundred thousand that no one else would know about. That's what I mean by protection."

Anthony handed Daniel a slip of paper with a bank account number. "Open this up." He had been watching this account for some time. Every month, two or three-hundred thousand dollars flowed through, with the balance never going below a half-million. Obviously, they used the bank to launder their money, and obviously the bank was complicit, because they deducted some very heavy fees.

Daniel hacked in and was stunned at the activity. He looked up at the boss's wife. "I can set up an offshore account for you with two-hundred thousand dollars.".

She looked surprised. "You can do that?"

"Right now, while we're waiting."

"What have I got to lose?"

Daniel called an international number using the hotel-room phone. With the information on her driver's license and her social security card, he set up a temporary account that would be good until the paperwork was finished. He transferred the money out of the New England syndicate account into the Genovese Family New York account, and from there into the boss's wife new offshore account. Once the two-hundred thousand was discovered missing, he could imagine the warm welcome they would receive if they called the

Genovese crime family. Daniel took a sheet of paper from the hotel note pad, wrote down the offshore account information, and handed it to the boss's wife. "Keep this safe," he said.

Anthony called the boss to check on his progress.

"Let me speak to my wife," said the boss.

"Yes, I'm all right," she said. "Did you find the girl?" She handed the phone back to Anthony. "He wants to talk to you."

After listening, Anthony put the phone down by his side. "They found Dark Angel, but there's a problem."

"What?"

"The guys who kidnapped her were paid by your two friends, Tom and Henry, who thought they could become rich overnight. What do you want to do?"

"I'll kill those bast…!"

"Just don't use a gun."

The boss's wife laughed. "These are your friends? And I thought we had problems."

Anthony brought the phone back to his ear. "I'll tell you what; send someone over to Tom and Henry to get their driver's licenses, social security numbers, car registrations, and VINs. And don't forget to tell your boys to let Dark Angel go."

"And bring Dark Angel here," said the boss's wife. "I want to see what all the fuss is about."

Twenty minutes later, there was a loud knock on the door. Daniel opened it to see Dark Angel standing there like it was just another Sunday afternoon. She walked in the room with the boss right behind her. His two men waited outside.

The boss's wife gave a nod of approval. "So, you're Dark Angel. Where'd you get a name like that?"

"It's a stage name," she said.

The boss took a closer look and remembered how he knew her but caught himself from saying anything in time to prevent his wife from adding to her list of grievances.

"Well, you're a beautiful girl," said the boss's wife. "They didn't bother you, did they?"

"They were pretty nervous about the whole thing. I don't think they knew what they were doing."

"You got that right." She looked at her husband. "Let's go, Frank. I've got to finish my shopping."

As soon as they left, Daniel returned to his laptop. He drained Tom and Henry's checking accounts, put a stop on their credit cards, and, with the help of Detective Anthony Duxbury, created an outstanding warrant for their arrest from the State of Florida. After all that hard work, they deserved a vacation, which would begin as soon as they were arrested for driving stolen vehicles.

Two weeks later Daniel received a phone call from the boss's wife asking if he could set up one of those accounts for a friend.

Perfect Crime

I don't know if you've ever made a mistake so horrible you prayed it would never be discovered or an error in judgment so incomprehensible it sends chills through your body, or been responsible for the lives of others and been found to be completely unreliable? I don't know if you can even imagine what it is like to have done, or been any of these, but I can tell you that, in my mind, I am all of these, and when I am unable to sleep at night, which is most of the time, I experience fear and loathing and wonder why my life had to happen the way it did.

Of course, two people traveling the same path and having the same experiences may view the journey differently. One might find it difficult to bear the weight of imprudence, while the other might shrug it off or hardly notice. Reactions also vary with the degree of impropriety ranging from a social indiscretion to unwarranted physical harm, and the individual's awareness of same, can range from hyper-sensitivity to all-embracing indifference.

My therapist says I am closer to the sensitivity point on the scale, and should be less critical of myself, but I think staying in bed for a weekend for fear of public ridicule for getting a parking ticket, is not irrational, and might even be considered prudent by some. My therapist also says, indirectly because I think he's shy, that I am naïve, unassuming and imperceptive, and that working on those issues would help me to understand why, last Wednesday afternoon I was sitting in a private dining room with my friends Arnie and Leon on the third floor of an old hotel with a large window overlooking Weybosset Street, waiting to be paid by Mr. Steele and Mr. Moretti for the work we did for them last Saturday night.

I met Mr. Steele two months earlier. He works in the Federal Building and is a very nice man. He gave me a few jobs, including transporting some of his friends from the airport to a hotel in my van when he was not available. He said he would be away for a while and asked me to meet him in New York to talk about a special job. Mr. Steele was kind enough to give me money for gas, parking, and a room, so I drove down two days later and parked my van in the hotel parking lot.

During a meal with Mr. Steele, he explained that he needed help in Boston, and if I had a couple of friends who wanted to earn some extra money, that would make the job a lot easier. He asked how much I knew about the cold war with Russia, and the spies they had planted in our country. He told me, in the strictest confidence, that some Russians broke into his Federal Building and stole boxes of gold and money. Mr. Steele said he and another agent, Mr. Moretti, had found where it was hidden, and planned to take it back next Saturday night if he could count on my help and the use of my van. This was to be an undercover operation, and because of that, I was sworn to secrecy.

After our meal, Mr. Steele mentioned he had some boxes of supplies that needed to be delivered back to Rhode Island and would I mind if they were put in my van. Of course, that was fine with me. He said thanks and gave me some money to enjoy New York. I had no idea the streets would be so crowded.

A week later, Arnie, Leon and I were sitting in that private dining room with wide oak floors and mahogany wall panels, at a table set with a burgundy-colored tablecloth, plates, glasses, and silverware for five people. The room had a single entrance, and the door was made of heavy oak that matched the interior paneling. On the opposite wall, you could look out through a large window to the street below. The dark-green curtains that hung on either side gave me a feeling of privacy and the sense of security I needed to help me with my fear of heights.

After waiting a few minutes, Mr. Steele and Mr. Moretti entered the room and sat down. A waiter followed with a pitcher of water and filled the glasses. He walked out and returned with a basket of bread and two shallow bowls filled with olive oil.

Mr. Steele and Mr. Moretti each took a sip of water, broke off a piece of bread, dipped it into the olive oil and took a bite before placing it on the small plate in front of them.

"Well, boys, how do you feel?"

"All right, Mr. Steele," I said, though noticing Leon's razor-thin smile, realized the words "all right" may have been premature.

"Good," he said, "I'm glad."

Mr. Moretti, a very large man, leaned forward. "You did what you were told and got us through a tight spot."

His words were gruff, and he most likely traveled in groups unknown to my friends and me, and we would never have met him if it weren't for Mr. Steele. Going from Mr. Steele to Mr. Moretti must be what's meant by a slippery slope.

Leon forced a smile and asked what was going to happen next, but I knew what he was thinking. *Now that we are here, when do we get paid and get to leave because, strange as it may seem, this isn't a lot of fun.*

"We just wanted to say thanks and wrap things up," said Mr. Steele. "No one likes the Russians and when we learned that their consulate was holding the stolen gold, thanks to you, we got it back."

Our job was to carry the stolen boxes of gold and bags of money from the consulate basement down a narrow alley off Arch Street to my waiting van under the supervision of Mr. Steele, while Mr. Moretti watched over us and provided direction.

When we were picking up a box inside the warehouse, a Russian came out of the dark, and threatened Arnie and me with a gun. I was too scared to move, but Mr. Moretti saved us by shooting him. There was little noise because Mr. Moretti used a silencer. He dragged the body into the basement behind some boxes, so we wouldn't have to look at it while we continued working.

Leon never found out until we returned home because he was loading the van when it happened, and it was not something I wanted to discuss on our way back to Providence. In fact, I don't even know when Mr. Moretti told Mr. Steele, because the subject never came up during the ride back.

"Gentleman," said Mr. Steele, "what would you like to eat? The waiter will be returning with a menu, but they will make up anything you want."

Before we could think of anything, the door swung open, and two large men entered the room and told Mr. Steele and Mr. Moretti to stand up. They spoke with Russian accents and were definitely not waiters. I don't mean to imply that people with Russian accents can't be waiters. I'm sure they would make very good waiters. It's just that in this case, they weren't.

One of the Russians held a gun that looked like the one used by the Russian in Boston that Mr. Moretti shot, and the other reached into Mr. Moretti's coat pocket and took his revolver while pushing both of them out the door. As soon as they were in the hallway, Mr. Steel grabbed the Russians holding the gun, but was shot by the second Russian holding Mr. Moretti's gun. He then turned to Mr. Moretti and shot him. *My God*, I thought, *he was shot with his own gun*. The Russians looked at us, then shut the door.

The three of us sat at the table scared to death. We looked at the window, which seemed to be our only hope. Making as little noise as possible we left our chairs and sort of crept across the room to the thick pane of glass and yelled for help until Arnie pointed out that since we couldn't hear the noise of the traffic up here, the pedestrians were unlikely to hear our yells for help down there. So, there we were, standing in front of the floor-to-ceiling window expecting to be killed at any minute with an unobstructed view of people walking along the sidewalk thirty feet below, and not one was looking up to watch us die.

I didn't know about Arnie or Leon, but I had been sweating so much, my pants were stuck to my legs and had to be pulled off my skin. I wiped my hands on the side of my shirt and stretched my shoulders back to relieve the cramp in my neck.

A few minutes went by without a sound from outside in the hallway and I wondered if there was a way to escape without being seen. Arnie looked at the door and then at me. What did he want me to do? Go out and get shot?

We reached the door at the same time, but I was closest, so I opened it as slow as possible. The hallway was empty, but the hard wood floor was wet with brown fluid, which could only have been the blood of Mr. Steele and Mr. Moretti. We walked around the puddles but didn't get far. The Russian who shot our friends stepped into the hallway, still holding Mr. Moretti's gun, and motioned us to turn around and go back inside. Without thinking, I walked right through the blood tracking it into the room. The Russian followed us and closed the door.

"We won't give you any trouble," said Arnie.

I guess not, I thought. How could we give him any trouble?'

I tried to think of a situation that could possibly be more dangerous. I could be hanging from the minute hand of a large clock

30 feet in the air or sitting in a car teetering over the edge of a cliff. That's all I could think of at that moment.

"Because you haven't shot us, does that mean everything's all right?" asked Leon.

The big man pulled out a chair, put his right foot on the seat, and pointed Mr. Moretti's gun at the three of us. "Why would you think everything's all right? Do you think you can steal from us and get away with it?"

This had to be the end. I was twenty-two years old, had wasted two years in college, failed at working in two factories, could not stomach the thought of sales, avoided a four-year commitment in the military and slid through life by hanging out and doing odd jobs. Yes, this was the end.

The big man moved forward and asked us what we thought when we killed his partner in Boston.

"We didn't kill him," I said.

"Moretti said you killed him with this gun."

"I've never seen that gun," I said, which wasn't true because I saw Mr. Moretti use it to shoot the Russian in Boston.

"This gun of yours killed my friend, and it just killed your partners; now I'm going to use it to kill you."

I could only hope for a quick and painless separation from Arnie and Leon and, of course, my earthly possessions. As he moved the gun closer to my chest, I experienced a calmness, while my friends pulled back in fear. I also wondered how Mr. Moretti told him I shot the Russian since he was already dead thanks to the Russian who was now threatening to kill me.

After a pause, he un-cocked the hammer and put the gun on the table. "I've got a better idea," he said. "If you want to live, you'll have to shoot your friends."

"What-the-hell! Are you kidding?" I said in disbelief. I didn't mean to swear.

"I don't know how to shoot a gun," I said without thinking, which was true, but you'd think my first thought would have been I can't shoot my friends, which I am sure Arnie and Leon would have preferred to hear me say. "And I'm not going to shoot my friends," I added, to make them feel better.

"I'll be outside. Pick up the gun and do it. If you don't, I'll come back an' kill you all. So, you two," pointing at Arnie and Leon, "you're gonna die either way." He left the room and closed the door.

This man is completely insane. I thought, and now Arnie and Leon were looking at me with fear and suspicion. I didn't blame them. Arnie's eyes darted back and forth between me and the gun. I couldn't move. I didn't want to move. Picking up the gun meant committing an unspeakable crime, and, worse, a sin, based on my recently disavowed Christian heritage.

"What are we going to do?" asked Arnie.

I walked back over to the window. It was thick and encased in a heavy wood frame sealed shut. I hit the glass with the side of my fist, and it didn't budge. Though, even if it did, not one of us would have had the courage to climb outside along the six-inch ledge to the rusty fire escape.

"Shoot him," said Leon almost under his breath.

"Shoot him," repeated Arnie.

This was a revelation. I couldn't shoot my friends, but maybe I could shoot the mad Russian. "Okay," I said, full of false bravado. "I'll shoot him when he comes in." I picked up the gun, which felt large and bulky in my hands. I had no idea what I was doing, but we had a plan. To overcome my nervousness, I walked around the table several times trying not to bump into the chairs or trip over my own feet. Arnie and Leon moved to a corner of the room away from the door. Another minute went by that seemed like an eternity, which I would guess they all do in such cases. I wanted to get this over with, so holding the gun in both hands I pointed the barrel up in the air and pulled the trigger. With a loud explosion, the bullet charged from the gun up into the ceiling. With the sound of the blast reverberating in my ears, the door swung open, and before I could move, the Russian grabbed the gun out of my hands, then pushed me down on the floor against the wall.

"I see you're playing games. Okay. Now you're going to die, and your friends go first."

With one hand, he grabbed Arnie by the neck and with the other grabbed Leon by his arm. He ran them out into the hallway and slammed the door shut.

Strangely, with everyone gone, my mind settled, and I began to think more clearly. But, looking up did make me a little dizzy, so I used a chair to pull myself off the floor and sat down at the table. The gun was four feet away, but by moving the chair sideways, I could reach down and pick it up without getting sick. I studied its lethal potential.

'No mistakes this time,' I thought. With all my strength and determination, I held it firmly with two hands, rested both elbows on the table, pointed the gun at the door, and waited for the Russian to walk into the room. They may kill my friends and even me, but at least one of them will pay with his life. I was determined, and it wasn't long before I had my chance.

The door opened, and the Russian walked into the room like nothing was going on. I don't think he even saw me until I pulled the trigger. His body barely moved. I fired two more shots. This time he fell backwards into the hallway. As he sank to the floor, I pulled the trigger one more time and heard a click. There were no more bullets, and for some reason, I remembered the count: three bullets for the

Russian, one for the ceiling, one for Mr. Moretti and one for Mr. Steele. The gun must have been a six shooter.

It was that easy. All you need is a weapon and the element of surprise, and you win every time. No matter how big or strong your opponent, no matter how threatening or frightening the situation. In the end, concentration, preparation, and steady nerves win the day. Although looking at a dead man you just shot is an unsettling experience, relief and gratification settle in to calm your nerves, that is, until fear of getting caught takes over, and once again you're on the run in hyper-drive.

I held the barrel of the gun with my shirtsleeve, so I could rub the grip with my pant leg to get rid of the fingerprints, and then dropped it on the floor. Now all I had to do was step over the dead body and not walk through any more blood. I don't remember doing any of this, but I do remember halfway down the hall a glowing red exit-light directing me to turn left into the stairwell. I ran down three flights, then stopped to catch my breath, hanging onto the railing to hold myself up. There were no voices, no footsteps, and no doors opening and closing. I continued down the half-flight of stairs to the rear of the lobby away from the elevators. In two minutes, I was in the parking lot unlocking my car door. Twenty minutes later, I was out of the city and in my apartment. No one followed me, and no one was inside waiting. Mr. Steele and Mr. Moretti were dead, and two Russians were dead all with the same weapon in less than a week. *Busy gun*, I thought.

After resting on the couch and calming my nerves, I realized I never heard the gunshots meant for Arnie and Leon, so maybe they got away. When I see them, I'd tell them I escaped, but there was no reason to tell them I killed the Russian. That would be too great a secret for anyone to bear, especially a friend.

My life of crime was over. And as far as I was concerned, it had never happened. I wanted my freedom to lead a productive and trouble-free life. The factories were still hiring, and if I cut my hair and cleaned up, I'd look as respectable as the next person standing in line for a job. The time is now, I thought. And then I fell asleep on my couch.

The next morning, I woke up to someone knocking on my door. One of the men introduced himself as Detective Martin from the Rhode Island State Police, and the other was Detective Hansen of the Massachusetts State Police. They knew my name and asked if they could come in.

Well, I thought, this whole thing may not be over, but at least I would be talking to an American.

Detective Martin said Arnie and Leon, went to the police station last night to report two men had been shot by Russians, who then tried to kill them, but they got away when the Russian left them alone to get you.

That about sums it up, except I had to make it clear that the money and the gold we took had been stolen from the United States Government by the Russians in the first place, and we were just getting it back to help our country.

The Massachusetts detective leaned forward and said, "What more can you tell us?"

I wasn't sure that I wanted to say any more, so I began by repeating everything they said. I told him that Mr. Moretti shot the Russian in Boston, and that's why the Russians came back to get even, and that I had escaped from the room right after my friends got away.

"Is that what happened?" asked State Trooper Hansen.

"Yes," I said.

"This is what I think happened," he said. "A week ago, you drove to New York, picked up boxes of stolen money, which we found in your basement yesterday afternoon, and last Saturday night, you went to Boston and stole boxes of guns from the McFadden Armored Truck Warehouse You and your friends met your partner and when you couldn't reach an agreement, you shot him in the chest and left him to die. We have the gun with your prints. Your story about Russian spies and a consulate is a fairy tale. There's no Russian consulate in Boston, and the only dead body is the one you shot."

I was so shocked; I didn't hear everything they said and never really understood what they were talking about. I do know they put me in handcuffs and drove me to the police station. With no money to post bail, that was the last I saw of the apartment and my worldly goods. I was charged with murder, grand larceny and transporting illegal weapons, though after murder, what difference does it make.

They had my fingerprints on the gun even though I had wiped them off, and the blood on the bottom of my shoes matched the blood, not of Mr. Moretti and Mr. Steel, but the man they said I shot, whose description sounded like the Italian waiter, even though I shot a Russian. They also said they found the man I killed inside the dining room by the window, not in the hallway. The bodies of Mr. Steele and Mr. Moretti were never found. The money I transported ended up in my basement, how I don't know, and no one knows anything about the gold in those boxes. They said they'd keep an eye out.

My friends Arnie and Leon did their best to tell their story to help me but were given immunity and coached on what to say. I would never say anything to put them in jeopardy because I was the one who asked them to come to Boston in the first place.

I was scared and filled with feelings of hopelessness and despair. For the mistakes I had made in my past, the errors in judgement that weighed heavily on my soul, and my inability to move forward, I will rightfully be spending the rest of my life in prison, but the punishment I receive, will be handed down for a crime I did not commit.

RHODE ISLAND 1982

GREATER GOOD

When Detective Martin asked me to meet him at the soccer field Saturday afternoon, it wasn't to watch teenage boys run up and down the field with more energy than Exxon or hang out with the local male population reaching the age of forty, a landmark he and I had shared years ago. We also shared a mutual appreciation for our separate jobs. He worked for the State police and was bound by layers of protocol but had access to an array of technology and support to solve crimes. I worked alone, free to investigate without oversight or court order, but had only my hunches to lean on. Years ago, I was on the force, but after a while, felt hemmed in and unable to breath.

I parked my car on the grassy bank and walked to the field with the other parents. We looked the same, except I was the one without a kid or a chair. I hoped the bleachers were softer than I remembered, because I knew that's where we'd be sitting.

Before I could reach the sidelines, my reason for being there caught my attention.

"Hello, Anthony. How've you been?"

"Hello, Detective Martin, nice to see you again. You got kids in the game?"

"Naw, I just enjoy the enthusiasm. Let's go up in the stands. You get a better view."

"You get a sore rear-end, too."

"If you had a little more padding like me, you wouldn't feel it so much."

We took a seat on a bench away from anyone who might be interested. Detective Martin always opened with the same question to soften me up.

"So, Anthony, how long were you on the force?"

"Seven years."

"Right. Anything you miss?"

"Yeah. I miss the excitement of pushing my way through a crowded room, flashing my badge, and arresting the bad guy. Even more, I miss the health benefits."

"In your seven years on the force, how many times did you push your way into a room flashing a badge?"

"Never."

"After twenty years, me neither."

By now the stands were filling up with enthusiastic parents and detective Martin motioned that we should move down a few feet, so we wouldn't be overheard.

"Speaking of bad guys, I heard you came into contact with Gerry Spyder."

I had to think about that. "Yeah," I said, "a couple of years ago, I guess it was."

"They say he was responsible for the death of Mattie O'Hare, one of the few forth-right politicians on the hill."

"He died in a car accident, didn't he?"

"That's what the report says, but why he rammed his car into the overpass is still a mystery. He could have fallen asleep I guess, or maybe this Spyder guy grabbed the wheel."

I had to think about that for a minute. "And walked away without a scratch?"

"You must have heard the rumor?"

Oh boy. Here it comes. "That Spyder couldn't die? That he's Dorian Gray?"

"After O'Hare's demise, the legislators passed a bill that took the pressure off the strip clubs."

"You saying O'Hare's death was a warning?"

"I think some politicians saw it that way. So, what can you tell me?"

I appreciated his choice of words, but in this case, there was no reason not to tell him the whole story. "It started when I got a call from a woman named Marion Marcello."

"Frank's wife? You working for the mob now?"

"Not yet," I said with a smile. "I helped her out once before. They had a teenage daughter involved with some kids doing drugs. Mrs. Marcello asked me to find her."

"How'd that go?"

"Easy. I talked to Howard, who was on drug detail at the time. He told me where the kids were hanging out. You should've seen the look on their faces when I broke through the door, flashed my badge, and grabbed the girl. One of the kids started screaming at me about who the girl's father was. When I told him the girl's father sent me, they scattered like scared rabbits, which they were."

"So, the one time you busted into a room flashing a badge you were impersonating a cop?"

"I guess. Anyway, Mrs. Marcello called. She claimed her husband was murdered, and since the police are prejudiced against the mob, they didn't spend much time looking for Frank's executioner, but not in those words." That got a smile out of Detective Martin. Some might call it a smirk, but I'll put him down for a smile.

"Listen," said detective Martin, "Frank Marcello was a mid-level bookie out with his girlfriend when he drove off the seawall. The car fell twenty feet, landing upside down on the rocks. He was cheating on his wife. If I were Marion Marcello, I wouldn't care how he died as long as he was gone. What did she want from you?"

"She called to meet for lunch."

*

Before I reached her table, Marion stood up to greet me. She was first class, forty- something stunning five-foot-four blond without a pound of extra weight. I was impressed.

"Hello Mr. Duxbury. Nice to see you again."

"How can I help you Mrs. Marcello?"

"You know about my husband, Frank, I suppose. He died in a car accident."

"Yes. I'm sorry for your loss."

"I lost him years ago. Don't feel sorry."

I nodded, trying not to smile.

"I'm sure you know how he made a living. He had friends. He had enemies."

"I understand he died in a car accident?"

"He was killed by a man named Gerry Spyder, a disgusting little man who hires himself out to kill people."

"An assassin."

"I wouldn't dignify him with such a title. He's a slimy rat. He kills because he can't get a job doing anything else. He just gets in your car and causes an accident."

"How does he do that?"

"I don't know. Maybe he has a gun and forces his way in. But once he's in, he causes the car to crash. Maybe he hides in the backseat. I don't know how he does it."

"Sounds suicidal to me."

"They say he can't die."

"We're all human. What would you like me to do?"

"I want you to find him and make him confess." Before I started to laugh, she stopped herself. "I guess that sounds ridiculous?"

I couldn't suppress a grin. "If life were that easy, Mrs. Marcello."

"I know. I know. Look, I just want you to find him and take care of things."

Great, now she thinks I'm a hit man. "Do you know where I can find him?"

Marion handed me a piece of paper with an address on it. "He lives there."

"What does he look like?"

"Short with black hair, thin, can't weigh more than 140 pounds."

Sounds like every hit man I've ever known, I thought. "May I ask why you never gave this information to the police?"

"I doubt they would've done anything. They weren't unhappy that my Frank was gone."

"And you think someone in the syndicate felt the same way?"

"I know they hired this Gerry to kill him."

I stood up to leave. "I'll call you when I have something."

The address Marion gave me was in a residential neighborhood. I drove out of the city to Spyder's house. It was a clean, modest white ranch with green shutters of questionable taste with a one-car garage, not at all fitting for a cold-blooded-killer.

There was a neighborhood elementary school around the corner with a large fenced in ball field. I parked down the street where I could get a rear view of Spyder's house. His back yard bordered the ball field's chain-link fence. There were large empty lots on either side of his property and the depth from the street to the fence was at least two-hundred feet.

There was nothing suspicious that I could see, and the backyard didn't look like a repository for missing persons. After twenty minutes, I drove to City Hall to find the owner of 23 Eden Crest Drive.

With help from a friendly clerk, I pulled the cards to learn that Spyder bought the house seven years ago, and later, bought the house lots next to him. I'll give you that he liked his privacy.

That evening I put a tracking device on his car, and after he drove off the next morning, I put a small camera inside the house. It wasn't long before I had his routine in my pocket. Except for an occasional trip to the basement, he came home from wherever, ate supper, watched TV, went to bed, got up, and left for the day. He ate out Friday nights. In all respects, he was a boring bachelor like the rest of us.

Next Friday night, right on schedule, Gerry returned to his favorite off-the-highway neighborhood restaurant and sat at the bar eating supper. He became more and more agitated as the night wore on. Those conversations in your head can be hell. Around 9:30, a man sat down next to him and ordered a drink. He and Spyder began a conversation that lasted twenty minutes. It was difficult to tell whether it was bar talk or the consummation of a contract. Either way, his happiness increased as the night wore on. By the time Gerry left, I could almost hear him whistle as he walked out the door.

The next afternoon I called Marion, because, so far, this case was going nowhere. She answered on the second ring as if she were waiting for my call and had nothing else to do, and that may have been the case.

"Hi, Mrs. Marcello. I've spent some time tagging along with Gerry Spyder. He hasn't done anything suspicious that I could see. Short, wiry guy with black-framed glasses, right?"

"That's the man who killed my husband."

"How do you know, Mrs. Marcello?"

"He killed my husband the same way he killed Mattie O'Hare."

"Mattie O'Hare the politician? How do you know that?"

"Because my husband was the one who set up the contract. Frank came home one night and told me I wouldn't believe what just happened. Said he was told to hire this guy, Gerry Spyder who thinks he's invincible. Best of all, Frank said, he's not connected, so no one would ever suspect, plus he guaranteed the death would look like an accident."

"If your husband hired him to kill O'Hare, why would he kill your husband?"

"Frank was next on the list; he just didn't know it. He got caught skimming. When you get caught, that's it. You're done. They paid Gerry to kill my Frank. Put him away Mr. Duxbury, anyway you can."

Next Friday night, while Spyder was enjoying the feel-good ambience of his favorite grille, I went inside his house with night goggles. The attic was clean. The first-floor furniture was nothing to look at unless you liked bland. The basement had an old bureau, a few cardboard boxes filled with kitchenware that should have gone out in the trash and a mirror leaning against the wall. A heavy oak table with a few chairs on top of a worn carpet sat in the middle of the floor. The oak table, I thought, he should keep that.

There was nothing here pointing to the killer described by Marion. I was half-way up the basement stairs when a car pulled into the driveway. By the time I reached the center hall, Spyder had his key in the lock. There's no place to hide in a small ranch, so I moved back to the spare bedroom closet. As a last resort, I could run him down and be out of the house before he knew what hit him.

Spyder flipped on the kitchen light and walked down the basement steps. I heard the table being dragged across the floor, and some other noises I couldn't make out. A few minutes later, I heard the table being moved again. Then he walked up the stairs and left the house.

Now, I'm wondering, what was Gerry Spyder doing in the basement? I went down the steps and moved the table and pulled the rug across the floor. Did I feel stupid. There was a bulkhead door, flush with the concrete floor, with recessed handles. I pulled it up to find six steps leading down to a steel door I didn't have the tools to crack so I hung a camera to give me an inside view the next time he unlocked the mysteries of life.

A few days later, I picked up the basement video. There was a partial view of a walk-in safe. I could see some money and a handgun. It was time to introduce myself to Gerry Spyder. In the meantime, I kept scanning the papers for accidental deaths of the rich and famous.

Next Friday, Spyder sat down at the bar, ordered the fish special, a draft beer and settled in for the evening. As the night wore on, and the customers played musical chairs until everyone had met the love of their life, I yelled across the bar to Gerry that we were the only ones left without a date. He laughed. By closing time, we were good friends. I asked him if he knew anyone who could help me with a business problem. He gave me his phone number. I called him Monday night, and we met Tuesday evening at his house.

"Here's the problem, Gerry. I have a successful business that someone is trying to take away from me. It would be worth a lot of money, a great deal of money, to get this guy off my back. I hope you won't mind if I don't tell you about the business."

"I understand," said Gerry. "I can handle it for you."

"That would be great. Who do you know?"

"I can handle it myself."

"Gerry, you're a good friend, but you don't seem the type..."

He became agitated, which was the reaction I was looking for. I asked him a few more questions until he became exasperated.

"Look," he said. "Remember that politician who went off the road? I did that. Remember the Mafia guy who drove off the sea wall? That was me. I can do anything."

"I thought those were accidents. Who wanted them dead?"

Gerry Spyder stopped. "I can't tell you that." He stood up from his chair and walked over to the living room window. He looked outside for a minute, maybe looking to see if we were alone, then turned back. "I'll tell you one of them because it doesn't make any difference. The one who paid me to kill that Mafia guy was his wife."

*

I looked over at Detective Martin: "So that's what I know about Gerry Spyder."

"You're telling me he confessed to murdering two people, and you didn't think to report that to the department?"

"Well, first of all, it seemed that everyone who hired Spyder to knock someone off, became Spyder's next victim, leaving no witnesses, until we come to Mrs. Marcello, who hired me to tie up loose ends, which I'm sure was for the good of the community."

"I'm sure. Maybe I'd better pay more attention to what you're doing. I didn't know you were cleaning up for the mob."

"I'm not, but I was faced with a moral dilemma."

"What moral dilemma?"

"I had to decide whether it was more important to rid the world of a sociopath who thought he discovered the fountain of youth or turn in a housewife who had almost every right to get rid of her scumbag husband."

"So, you chose door number one."

"It seemed the right thing to do. So, I convinced Gerry that my job would be the biggest of his life, worth over half-a-million, but that he'd have to leave town after it was done. I suggested Brazil, with its limited extradition treaty. He'd be living in a warm climate with plenty of money. I also convinced him he would be remembered as an upstanding citizen if he took down his house, built a soccer field on his three lots, and gave it to the town. And that's exactly what he did. And you know that oak table in my office? Gerry gave it to me for all my trouble."

"You're an amazing guy, Anthony. So where is this soccer field?"

"Right here, detective. You're practically sitting on Gerry Spyder's front steps."

"You're kidding, right?"

"No, I'm not. It's a great field don't you think?"

"And where is Mr. Spyder?"

"He's around somewhere. He claimed to be the undying sort."

"You don't believe that, do you?"

"Who am I to judge?"

"Okay, where is he?"

"Given his extraordinary skill for extrication, he could be on the beach in Rio de Janeiro with the other tourists, or…"

"Or what?"

"Or he could still be inside his safe waiting for someone to unlock the door.

Rhode Island 1986

Guilty Party

Private Investigator Anthony Duxbury had made a name for himself for putting away Gerry Spyder, a one-man crime wave that couldn't be stopped by normal means. Not that Duxbury's name could be found in print or on the lips of local newscasters, but it circulated where it mattered most: among the police, in the courts, and with the attorneys: everywhere it counted when you needed a referral to put food on the table.

And it was in the Second District Court third floor hallway where Dr. Warren, a forensic psychiatrist, while waiting three hours to testify at the trial of an elderly gentleman who had been directed by an inner voice to assault those who offended him, overheard the Duxbury legend. Dr. Warren thought that if the story were even half true, a man of such ingenuity, might be able to help one of his patients. He called Duxbury's office the next day and left a message requesting an appointment on a confidential matter.

Two days later Dr. Warren stood outside the door with the initials ADPI printed on the glass. He rang the bell and stepped inside. The anteroom held four chairs, a small table, and coat rack. Before he could sit down, the second door opened, and Anthony Duxbury ushered him inside to a comfortable chair in front of a solid oak table that belonged in someone's dining room, but now served as a desk and conference table. Anthony sat down in a chair on the opposite side and asked how he could help.

"I have a client, a young man named Jonathan Spence, awaiting trial in prison, charged with stealing money from a warehouse and shooting his partner."

"Must be a tough customer if they didn't set bail."

"They did, and he should be out, but he has no financial resources."

"Is the partner dead?"

"I'm afraid so."

"Who was his lawyer?"

"A public defender named DeMagistris."

"Don't know him, and the case doesn't sound familiar either."

"It happened in Boston and hasn't been on the news."

"Boston?" Anthony stretched his arms behind his back. His six-foot frame gave the appearance of strength and restlessness as it more than filled the chair. He did not take cases in Boston, plus the Massachusetts Attorney General was running for re-election and wouldn't look kindly upon being overturned a few weeks before the voters reached the polls.

"Who brought him in?"

"He was arrested by a Massachusetts State Trooper with the help of the Rhode Island State Police."

"Why Rhode Island?"

"That's where he shot the man in self-defense."

"His partner tried to kill him?"

"No. A Russian tried to kill him for witnessing a murder, but my patient killed him first."

"So, he was charged with killing a Russian?"

"No. They never found the Russian. He was charged with killing an alleged partner."

The story was getting complicated, so he decided he'd better read the police report before he went any further.

"Do you have the name of the Rhode Island detective?"

"Yes." Dr. Warren reached into his jacket pocket for a small note pad and turned a few pages. "His name is Detective James Martin."

Anthony smiled. He hadn't seen his friend for almost a year. This would give him an excuse to call.

Dr. Warren returned the notepad to his inside pocket and looked pleadingly at the private investigator. "I guess what I'm asking is, would you talk to my patient just to hear what he has to say? He has no interest in standing up for himself, which is part of the problem."

"A pretty big one, I'd say."

"Yes, it is. I'll be responsible for your time."

"Let me make sure I understand. Your patient stole money in Boston, shot someone in Rhode Island, and is being held in Massachusetts."

"He's at the Walpole State Prison."

Since murder took precedence over robbery, Anthony wondered why Spence was not locked up in Rhode Island. He agreed to the visit and told Dr. Warren he'd get back to him.

Duxbury called Walpole to arrange a time, and then left a phone message for Detective Martin that he'd won a free lunch for any day next week in exchange for anything he knew about Jonathan Spence.

Walpole Prison was a great example of what could be done with a fresh coat of paint and a new administration. But the best part about Walpole for Duxbury was, he could get there in thirty minutes from his office.

Twenty minutes later, he drove off the highway onto the old Boston Post Road where he noticed a large tract of vacant and abused land along the Foxboro line that he thought could be developed into a mall or a football stadium if he only had the money. Unfortunately, there were no entrepreneurial genes in his family, which is why he kept his head down and nose to the grindstone.

Jonathan Spence was sitting behind a table in a small interview room, his wrists and ankles shackled. He was twenty-two years old and looked even younger; no more than five-feet six, weighing less than a hundred and forty pounds. He looked like he belonged in prison as much as the Easter Bunny belonged on top of a Christmas tree. Anthony requested the guard remove Jonathan's hardware. After the guard left, he explained that Dr. Warren asked him to visit, and that he was here to listen to what he had to say.

"I helped Mr. Steele and Mr. Moretti carry boxes of gold stolen from our government out of the Russian Consulate in Boston. Mr. Moretti shot a Russian guard and we left."

"I thought you were the one who shot the guard."

"No. I shot a different Russian in Providence who was trying to kill me."

"That was the body the police found?"

"No. They said I shot one of the gang members because that's the body they found. But there was no gang; it was just my friends and me working for Mr. Steele and Mr. Moretti."

Anthony pulled out a pad and tried to suppress a smile. "You're not making any of this up, right?"

"I know how it sounds," said Jonathan, "but it's true. After we took the gold, we met in a Harrington Hotel dining room on the third floor. Before Mr. Steele and Mr. Moretti could pay us, two men came in. They said we'd stolen their money. They shot Mr. Steele and Mr. Moretti, then came back to kill us. He gave me a gun and told me to shoot my friends and when I didn't, he took them out of the room. When he came back for me, I shot him."

"In self-defense?"

"Yes."

"How many shots did you fire?"

"Four: one at the ceiling and three at the Russian."

"So, who was the gang member, they said you shot?"

"I don't know. They found some guy inside the room I never heard of."

Anthony had been on this track before with the psychiatrist and wanted to get off.

"Mr. Spence. I'd like to talk to your friends."

"They were just helping me move some boxes. Everything is my fault, not theirs.

"You feel guilty?" asked Anthony.

"Of course. I can't sleep at night thinking about what I put them through."

"But you're in here, and they're out there. What's done is done. You're the one getting punished, not them."

"Do you believe in karma?"

"It hasn't worked for me."

"I believe I've made some mistakes in my life and am being punished for them. Besides I did kill someone; I just don't know who. So maybe this is where I belong."

"Jonathan," said Anthony, "in this country the justice system says you don't go to jail for a crime you didn't commit," I lied. "But I have to ask. If they're charging you with murder in Rhode Island and robbery in Massachusetts, why aren't you in a Rhode Island prison?"

"I don't know. They never told me. Maybe because the robbery came first? I don't know."

Duxbury left the prison with the names and phone numbers of Arnie and Leon, whom he would call that night after a quick search of their background. They might have robbed the Russian Consulate in Boston, but if they were anything like Jonathan Spence, they probably had no idea what they were doing.

It didn't take long for Duxbury to learn that Arnie had his own apartment and Leon was still living at home with his parents. He decided to wait until 8:00 pm when most people were in for the night. Arnie picked up the phone on the second ring.

"Hello. This is Mr. Duxbury. Are you Arnie? Jonathan Spence gave me your number. You a friend of his?"

"Yes. I know him."

His caution was unmistakable. If Spence's story was true, Arnie and Leon went through a lot of unnecessary grief, and for all Duxbury knew, it could have been more pressure than a friendship could bear. They had a right to be cautious, even suspicious.

"I'm a private investigator who was asked to help Jonathan. I met with him earlier today."

"Okay."

"I'd like to meet with you and Leon. Would you two be available sometime during the week or on the weekend?"

"I'd have to call Leon, but probably the weekend would be better."

"Talk to Leon and come up with something. I'll buy lunch. Your friend Jonathan is a nice kid. I'd like to help him." Duxbury called the next night, and they agreed to a Sunday brunch.

After they shook hands and sat down, Anthony learned that Arnie was working in sales for a New-Jersey- based grocer opening stores in New England. He seemed intelligent enough and had absolutely no reason to be involved in a robbery. His friend Leon had no reason either. He was learning to become a manager for a small chain of bookstores. Both of their futures looked bright, even though their recent past had a minor blemish. They had just been dragged unknowingly into a swamp to take the fall for someone who knew more about life's underbelly than the three of them together would learn in a lifetime, but they'd get over it.

Anthony didn't want this to become a therapy session, so he got right to the point.

"You boys took stolen gold from the Russian Consulate?"

"That's what Jonathan told us," Said Leon.

"Explain."

Arnie looked at Leon, who gave him the go ahead. "Jonathan asked us to help him and two other guys move boxes into his truck. Me and Jonathan were carrying them out of the building to the van and Leon was stacking. Some guy came out of the building and Mr. Moretti shot him. A couple of days later we met at a hotel to get paid. Two Russians showed up, shot Steele and Moretti, and threatened to shoot us, but we got away when we were left alone on the stairwell. Jonathan shot the man coming back to get him, but we weren't there when it happened."

"Jonathan had a gun?"

"The guy gave Jonathan a gun and told him to shoot us."

"Well," said Anthony, "you must be glad he didn't."

This didn't elicit even the faintest smile, so he continued. "We've got four missing bodies; two Russians, Steele and Moretti. And a fifth body no one has ever heard of. Doesn't this all sound a little strange to you?"

The boys began to relax as the absurdities piled up.

"What'd the police say?"

"We went to the police station to tell them what happened. They didn't really believe us, but when they came back, they were pretty upset. They took our statement and told us to go home and not talk to anyone until we heard from them."

Why would the police be upset about a dead body? wondered Anthony. They see them all the time. "So, Jonathan was arrested and sent to prison. How did you get off?"

"The police came back and told us we'd only be asked about the robbery. They said the murder charges would come up later and we'd get immunity."

"Can I ask you a question about your friend Jonathan? You don't have to answer if you don't want to. What kind of guy is he? Is he capable of committing a crime or was he duped?"

"We were all duped," said Leon.

"We were dopes," said Arnie.

"These guys, Steele and Moretti, you think you'd recognize them if you saw them again?"

"If they're alive. I don't like looking at dead people," said Leon.

Duxbury took out a note pad. "Give me a description?"

When he finished, Duxbury drove back to the city to see where all this shooting took place and found plenty of parking behind the old hotel.

The building was a founding-father's original that had been refurbished and repainted more times than the face of a city hooker, but after a while, you can do just so much. An outdated restaurant and bar occupied the first floor and saw most of its customers between noon and seven when it was time for the patrons to go home or off to their next adventure. The second floor was used for an occasional private party, but the rooms had not been updated in years and any building in the city less than twenty years old looked fresher. On this Sunday afternoon, there were six people in front of the bar and one behind.

Duxbury grabbed a flashlight from the glove compartment and made his way to the men's room then continued down the hall to a set of stairs that took him to the third. The police tape was easy to spot, and the door was unlocked. There was nothing inside except an old dining room table and six chairs. The room was too dirty for private parties, and he guessed its only use was to stage a crime and dump a body. Duxbury played his light around the ceiling and saw that it had not been touched by either a fresh coat of paint or a bullet from Jonathan's gun.

Later that evening, with the descriptions of Steele and Moretti inscribed in his mind, he stopped by Club Magic to see if anyone looked familiar. After an hour of nursing one beer the magic had worn off and seeing no one coming close to either description, he walked out the door leaving the bartender underemployed then drove to one more club on the waterfront, but the results were the same.

Three things bothered Duxbury: no bodies, no bullet holes, and no gold. First thing tomorrow morning he'd look up DeMagistris to see what he was doing with the case.

Anthony could have made an appointment, but if he got there early enough, he'd catch them with their first cup of coffee and get what he needed without being escorted out the door. Duxbury knew there was no group of public servants swimming upstream against a stronger current than these lawyers, as evidenced by the restrained emotional qualities and dark sense of humor required to survive the dusty labyrinth of law and prejudice they negotiated every day. Federal funds and the promise of a better tomorrow extended the enlistment time for some, but service was short for most.

He slipped past the unmanned receptionist's desk and walked down the hall to the coffee room, right across from the copy center closet. He did have one friend in the department who could have retired but stuck around for the oxygen and enthusiasm brought in by the young lawyers.

Duxbury walked into the room and asked for Henry Jenks and an attorney named DeMagistris. A kid who looked like a high school intern said he hadn't seen Henry this morning, but he was DeMagistris. Duxbury apologized and said he meant the trial lawyer. The kid assured him he was the trial lawyer. Anthony was at a loss for words as the young attorney with too much energy and a fresh smile led him out of the room to a corner desk and invited him to sit down.

DeMagistris pulled up a chair next to Anthony and laughed: "I get that a lot from you old guys. What's up?"

Duxbury took out his identification and said he was working on a case. "You represented Jonathan Spence?" he asked.

"Yes, but he really needs a full-time attorney. I think Mr. Spence is innocent, but he won't help himself, and I don't have the time to go digging through records to find the missing pieces."

"I saw him at Walpole, and he needs more than a lawyer. He told me he believes in karma and that's why he's in prison."

"If karma existed, you could make an argument that the justice system isn't needed. Why'd you ask for Henry Jenks?"

"In case the receptionist tried to throw me out for not having an appointment, he's the only one I know who might defend me."

"Yeah, Doris would do that. I have to be in court at nine for a pre- trial before a judge who's never more than an hour late, so we've got five minutes."

"I need to find two guys named Steele and Moretti."

"The elusive ones. I know. I couldn't get Spence interested in helping us out."

"I think his friends Arnie and Leon would do it. Can we get access to mug shots?"

"Sure. I can call the state police, and they'll set it up."

"I think they're from Boston, which is why nobody seems to know them."

"Out-of-towners. In that case, you need your friend Henry to pull the strings."

Duxbury got up and thanked DeMagistris. "What time does Henry get in?"

Before he could answer, a man grabbed him by the arm. "Hello Anthony Duxbury. What brings you down here so early?" Henry's timing was perfect, but even better, agreed to arrange for Arnie and

Leon to spend a morning in Boston looking at the black and whites of those who didn't get away.

It took the boys a while to identify Steele and Moretti, and it was by luck they were in the book because their last known address was New York City. They were picked up in Boston with a canvass bag full of handguns. The police suspected they had been stolen from one of the smallover-seas factories, but suspicion was not enough to make a case, so they were sent on their way minus the weapons.

Arnie and Leon flipped through a few more pages of black and whites then stopped. "That's the Russian guard Mr. Moretti killed in Boston."

The Russian had been convicted of transporting guns into the country for which he got six-months suspended. He wrote down his last-known address, thanked the officer behind the desk, and told the boys he was buying lunch, for a second time.

Knowing these people don't travel far from the roost without getting paid, Duxbury drove to the Russian's neighborhood and found the closest deli. He ordered some sandwiches and handed them to the boys who were sitting in a corner booth. "If this guy walks through the door, keep your heads down and don't look surprised." A half-hour later the dead Russian came in and ordered smoked turkey with bacon on pumpernickel. The boys played it cool and did as they were told.

After the Russian left, they drove over to Arch Street. Duxbury parked the car, so the boys could show him the alley they used to get into the Russian Consulate. Duxbury walked down the side of a brick building until he came to a steel door that looked impenetrable and unscratched. A small sign said McFadden Warehouse. So much for the Russian Consulate. He wondered who opened the door from the inside.

On their way back to Providence, they stopped at Walpole State Prison. Anthony had prearranged a visit and hoped the reunion would spark some life into Jonathan. This time the interview room was a little larger, and he came in without the shackles. After greeting each other and telling Jonathan they saw the Russian guard that was shot by Mr. Moretti, his vital signs returned to normal.

"Now that you three are together, I want you to think about those boxes you were carrying. How heavy would you say they were?"

"A little. Not too much," said Leon

"You agree, Jonathan?" asked Duxbury.

Jonathan nodded his head yes.

"I don't think you were carrying gold; I think you were carrying guns, which were probably on their way to different gangs across the country. You said you met Steele in New York City. Did he give you anything to bring back?"

"Just some supplies."

"I'm sure they were. Do any of you know this man?" he pulled out a morgue photo of the dead man found inside the hotel's private dining room.

"That's the waiter who brought water into the room," said Jonathan.

"That's the man they said you shot."

"I didn't shoot him. I shot a Russian."

Duxbury dropped the boys off at Arnie's apartment, thanked them and drove to Providence where he made a phone call and then took the last train available to New York City.

Penn Station was empty after midnight, except for Anthony's friend who guided him along the streets to Steele's last known address. They saw a plain brick building on a quiet corner with clean sidewalks, and a small coffee shop that looked like it would be a good place to have breakfast in about six hours.

Duxbury and his friend began sipping their first cup of coffee by 7:10 and continued, somewhat conspicuously until 8:45, reading, and re-reading, the newspaper until they saw Steele walk out of the building. Anthony looked up and positively identified him as being alive and without an obvious bullet hole. "I guess that's it," said Anthony.

"You come all the way to New York just to say that's it? Where's your due diligence? You go follow Steele and meet me back here in an hour."

"What are you gonna do?"

"Never mind me; go before you lose him."

Anthony had no trouble keeping up. For a New Yorker, Steele didn't walk very fast. He turned the corner and continued along Third Avenue to a deli where he joined Moretti and two other men whom Anthony felt sure had found their way into more than one police line-up. He walked across the street and sat down at the bus stop to wait. A half-hour later, they left the deli, and Anthony returned to the coffee shop to meet his friend.

"This is for you."

"What is it?" asked Anthony.

"It's a notebook I found in Steele's apartment that should help get your client out of jail."

Friday morning's clear sky gave hope for a much-needed warm spring day, but the sun's rays were never a match for the north wind, so Duxbury wore his windbreaker just in case. By 11:30, he was in a restaurant sitting across from his friend detective James Martin.

"How'd you get involved in the Spence case?"

"His therapist asked me to talk to him because he wouldn't defend himself."

"Maybe he's guilty?"

"He's guilty of something, but I don't know what, and I don't think he does either. Do you have any idea why the news hasn't caught up with this story?"

Detective Martin picked up his cup of coffee and drank slowly then returned the cup to the table without saying a word.

Duxbury took up the slack. "Nod, if I strike a chord. Spence didn't kill anyone?" Martin nodded slightly. "The man you found had no connection with my client." Martin nodded again. Duxbury decided to push the boundaries. He could think of only one reason the police would keep someone's death out of the news and were on edge. "The dead man was an undercover cop?"

Martin lowered his head. "Yes," he said.

"Sorry. That's rough. Well, they're not gonna convict Spence of killing an undercover cop. All he has to do is appear in court with his baby face and the jury will acquit before the opening statement."

"It's a problem. The kid was in the wrong place at the wrong time."

"Do you know a Steele and Moretti?"

"Their names are in the report, but we haven't found them."

"Spence saw Steele, Moretti and a Russian from Boston get shot. But the fact is all three are walking around in good health, which is just as strange as a hotel ceiling that took a bullet without leaving a hole, which I'm sure you already know. I think everyone was playing cowboys and Indians, shooting blanks for Spence's entertainment. Then they gave him the same gun to make him think he killed someone. I doubt he could hit either one of us if we were three feet away. Where did they find the body?"

"Inside the dining room against the back wall."

"And Spence says the guy he shot was in the hallway."

"I read the report. Where'd you see Steele?"

"Outside his New York walk-up."

"He see you?"

"Could have, but he has no idea who I am." Anthony pulled out a notebook and handed it to Martin. "You can have this."

"What is it?"

"Steele's contacts and gun sale records."

"You should give this to Boston; it's their case."

"You give it to Boston, then they'll owe you a favor."

"Thanks."

"We know everyone involved except the two missing Russians, and I'm guessing one of them pulled the trigger. Steele and Moretti know who they are since they were play acting together. How do you shoot a gun with someone else's prints on the handle without leaving your own?"

"Latex glove. Keeps your prints off without removing the old ones."

"And did you find the gloves?"

"No."

"But they don't know that. Why don't you bring them all in at the same time, so they can see each other? Let them know it's a federal crime; you could even get one of your FBI friends to let you borrow a room in the federal building. I'll do surveillance on the Boston Russian and find a couple of his friends to drag in with him. Show Steele his notebook. Start with gunrunning and end with murder. Let them know you need a name if they want to be home for the holidays."

A week later two New York State troopers delivered Steele and Moretti to the federal building at the same time a Massachusetts state van delivered the Russian with three of his friends; they also delivered Spence. Everyone walked in together and were given plenty of time to make eye contact before moving on to separate rooms. With the death penalty on the table, by 1 pm, they had a name and by 4 pm, he was cuffed in the back of a trooper's car on his way to the Rhode Island State Penitentiary. He used blanks to shoot Steele and Moretti but used real bullets to shoot the under-cover police officer, and since he drove over the state into little Rhody to commit the crime, the Feds had the death penalty on the table quicker than you could drive from one end of the state to the other.

In addition to the death penalty for one, and conspiracy charges for all, there were enough laws broken that, everyone came away with an updated rap sheet.

Jonathan Spence was set free. It was true he transported stolen money from New York and illegal weapons from Boston over the state line into Rhode Island and both were federal crimes, but they were committed unknowingly, and for that, he was not punished, which says a thing or two about Karma after all.

Border Crimes

Pritchard's Garage, on Brown Street, behind the main drag in Narragansett, was one of those comfortable places people would go just to hang out. It was a shop you could drive into without an appointment to get any part of your car adjusted, repaired or replaced without delay as long as the only tools required were a socket wrench, screwdriver, pliers or hammer. It was that way when it opened after World War II and is that way today if you're a regular. The garage is two connecting wooden structures sitting fifty feet off the road fronted by an unpaved lot made up of hard-packed gravel and soft sand.

It was not unusual to drive in for a minor problem and before you get out of your car, have someone pop the hood, listen intently, go back to the garage for the right tools, make an adjustment and gently return the hood to its cradle. Only when you tried to pay, did you learn that your car had been fixed by a knowledgeable customer waiting for theirs to be repaired by one of the mechanics inside.

On a warm August morning, John eased his 235 cubic-inch inline-6 five-year old 54 Chevy Bel Air Sports Coupe onto the gravel parking lot fronting Pritchard's garage for an oil change, grease-job and a fluid check. There was only one other car ahead of his.

John worked for a small South County publishing house that was always looking for their next book project, which was his job to find and edit. An English major from a prominent college who did not share his classmates' illusion of writing the next great American novel, he opted instead for the daily grind of editorial work that would hopefully lead to a financially secure position in one of the bigger houses where he would be reunited with his classmates, but from the business side of the editor's desk. Or, if a lost relative left him an inheritance, he could buy the Blue Heron Press and live blissfully in South County with a view of the sand dunes and Atlantic Ocean for the rest of his life.

One day, John suggested to his boss, that the Blue Heron publish a book of photographs detailing life in two or three small New England towns touching the Canadian border. The publisher-owner, a prudent, wise gentleman, thought the book might generate interest throughout New England and even some southern states where people had a penchant for small town life. John further suggested that a way to save money and create publicity, would be to give the Providence Arts College a grant to be awarded to a senior or recent graduate who submitted the best landscape photography proposal, and use the East Side Photo Lab to print the photographs, which they would display in their foyer at the time of publication.

The owner liked the idea, and in truth liked John very much as well. In fact, he saw in John someone who could take over the Heron and eventually buy the company, which he was ready to sell.

The owner had done well during the last twenty-three years with regional publishing, but the time had come and the heir apparent, his only son, Thompson, did not have the drive or patience to see a project through. And growing up with financial means, had wrapped himself inside a false sense of entitlement squandering his time and money on alcohol and drugs to the shame and dismay of his parents.

By Thursday afternoon the owner and John specked out and budgeted the book. He called East Side for an appointment with the brother who handled the business end of the company. Both knew

John and had done work for the Blue Heron in the past. A meeting was set for Friday.

John finished the proposal and locked the doors around five. The sun was still above the horizon, April was coming to an end, and the south-west prevailing winds were warm enough for John to shed his winter jacket, but never farther than arm's length. He lived twenty minutes from home if he drove the back roads and side streets.

He parked his Chevy in a garage he rented one house down from his first-floor apartment. After shutting down the stove-bolt six, he listened for any instructive sound that would give warning to future mechanical problems as the engine settled in for the night. Hearing none, he walked back to the side entrance of his apartment that led directly into the kitchen. After hanging his jacket on a hallway peg he entered the living room, pushed aside the white lace curtains inherited from the previous tenant and looked out the front window across the street.

Neither the two-story Victorian painted to the nines on his left nor the gray colonial with mandatory white trim on the right was of interest at 5:30 that afternoon, but the sixty-foot space between them was, for it provided an open view of Main Street, and a parking lot that led to the harbor with a view of sailboats moored on either side of the channel. During the summer months John sat on the porch to watch the cars and pedestrians travel from left to right or right to left across this stage without realizing they were summer stock for an audience of one. The mix seldom deviated from an eighty/twenty assortment of tourists and locals.

This early in the season, there were few people out, so he decided to call his friend Arne Sikes with the good news. He and Arne graduated together from the same high school and remained friends ever since even though they attended different colleges. They kept in touch by using school breaks to share hopes, hardships, and cemented their bond with minor sacrifices for each other during the years that followed. Arne had completed college with a major in photography and was working for a prominent studio doing weddings, the bread, butter and boring side of photography, and a little glamour work to pay for his expensive hobby, large-format landscape photography.

John picked up the phone and dialed.

"Hello," said a sweet voice.

"Hi Q. It's John. How are you?"

"John, I love it when you call" she said.

"It's a pleasure to hear your voice too, and you're looking well I might add. Any chance Arne is available to come to the phone?"

"No, unfortunately. Our mutual and recently married college professor friend is at the hospital with his wife who is giving birth to their first, so Arne is on campus covering his class. It'll be a night in the dark room trying not to dissolve his fingers in chemicals."

"The baby came quick."

"They say the first one can come at any time but, strangely, all the others take nine months.

"What's he doing this weekend?"

"Earning his keep. He's got a bridal party shoot tomorrow night and the wedding on Saturday. Why don't you come over Sunday afternoon? He'll be up by then and I'll make something to go with the red wine you bring."

"Red wine. Got it."

"So now that your weekend is open, why don't you go down to the Oaks for a drink and say hello to my friend Millie. I know she'd like to see you again."

"I might. Anyway, I'll see you Sunday. Thanks."

The next morning, he left for Providence. The East Side Photo Lab was established seventy-five years ago to provide film, processing and prints for professional photographers. It also had the capacity to provide plates for magazine and book publishers. The building contained a thirty-by-forty lobby where large prints of local artists could be displayed during their monthly gallery nights.

The receptionist led John through the main office, carpeted in soft blue, into the conference room with wide-board pine flooring. The walls were painted light gray, which caused the photographs to jump out. Color had become the new medium, expensively replacing black and whites. Three minutes later the older brother came in greeting John warmly.

John explained the pre-and-post publicity aspects of publishing a book of small-town photographs that East Side would print and display during a combination gallery night and book release. Heron Press would provide money for a grant to the Art College they could use to fund a photographer for the project. The brother thought it was a good idea and asked what the college thought. John explained this was his first stop and he'd approach the college next.

"How much time do you have?" the older brother asked.

"Some."

"Excuse me for one moment,"

Three minutes later the older brother returned to the conference room. He had called David Eldridge, head of the photography department, and they were meeting him for lunch in twenty minutes.

They found David in the student cafeteria and grabbed an empty table next to a window overlooking a small quad. John looked outside to what could only be described as a wide assortment of multi-faceted students exuding a megaton of energy dressed in the most diverse and eclectic ensembles imaginable. The view was exhilarating.

John thanked Dr. Eldridge for seeing them and explained the idea for the book, East Side's involvement and the proposed grant award to a graduate or recently graduated student working in the field of landscape photography. Dr. Eldridge said he thought the idea had merit and looked forward to the written proposal. They spent another five minutes talking about the school before Dr. Eldridge had to return to his studio.

Back at the Blue Heron, John completed the book proposal and put it in the mail to East Side Photo and the Arts College, before he called it quits for the weekend. Later that evening he would take Q's suggestion and visit Millie at the Oaks.

The Oaks was an established South County favorite watering hole for locals and college students. By 10:00 pm, there were few seats left. John drove his Bel Air to the back of the lot off to one side on a slight embankment into the only parking spot left. He found his way to the bar and paid for a beer, then pressed his way through warm bodies until he reached the back of the room and sat down at a small empty table. Before he had a chance to relax, he was joined by a slightly disheveled man in his late twenties he had met only once before.

"So, are you gonna buy the Blue Heron Press?" said Thompson.

Before John could think he said, "What are you doing here?" He wanted to ask him why he wasn't out doing drugs with his friends but knew nothing good would come of that. As much as he disliked the son of the man who owned the Blue Heron, there was no value in letting him know how he felt.

Thompson took a sip of his beer then smiled. "You're a bright light in my father's eye which is more than you can say for me. My father wants to retire and you're the only one he'd trust to take over."

John was surprised by his candid remarks.

"I don't have the money to buy the Heron."

"There's always ways to get money. And besides my mother says you got good ideas for books. You could probably make it up in a couple of years."

"What do you know about the business?"

"A lot more than you think."

The waitress brought a second round and they talked for a while until Thompson decided to leave.

John sat upright in his chair and raised his arms over his head to stretch, when another hand brought his right arm down and around the waist of the waitress standing next to him.

"I'm glad all my customers aren't this forward," she said.

John looked up. "Millie?"

"Hi," she said, with a smile that was difficult to forget.

"I didn't see you when I came in."

"I'm working the back room an' just came out for a break."

"Who's in there?"

"Locals. Loud and proud of course, but they know the score."

"What's the score?"

"The score is, I'm one and they're zero. The beer keeps coming as long as they stick to their girlfriends and buddies."

John laughed. "Well, I am glad you're taking care of yourself."

"I see you were talking to your boss's son."

"You know him?"

"Everyone knows Thompson. And everyone I know stays away."

"I didn't come here to meet him, that's for sure. Actually, I was talking to Q earlier and thought I'd come by and say hello to you."

Millie cocked her head sideways, bent slightly at the waist and looked him in the eyes. "Stay around to closing, and you can do just that."

"I might," he said.

By one o'clock Sunday afternoon John was on his way to East Providence where Arne shared an apartment with Q just one block off the Boulevard with its well-known broad grassy median that becomes an improvised park and jogging trail seven months a year. They shared the apartment expenses, and each had their own bedroom though by Q's admission sometimes a girl gets lonely; however, her intentions were quite clear.

Q worked in a teaching-hospital lab because she was holding out for a doctor. She was a twenty-four-year-old microbiology grad student with a dark complexion, darker eyes, black hair, well-developed features and a quick smile. She had many suitors including a judge living in the area; but her heart was set on a GP who would be satisfied with one wife and two children. She had already tapped Arne to be the photographer and John to be the ring bearer. Q's real name was Marissa Morel, but for reasons best known to her, she preferred to be called Q.

John parked his Bel Air in front of the two-family white shingled colonial, rang the top doorbell, opened the front door and walked up the wooden stairs. The apartment door had been left open. "Hello," he yelled.

Arne greeted him as he came through the door. "Come on in. I am just putting my gear away." His camera bag open, and he was carefully packing up his Hasselblad, which cost more than the car John was driving, two camera backs and an assortment of lenses and filters. The exposed rolls of film were in a black bag. Monday morning, he would bring them to the photo lab to print contact sheets.

"How was the wedding?"

"Wonderful. Between keeping the drunken brother from stepping in front of my shots and posing a bride with asymmetrical breasts to look elegant, it was absolutely super."

"Did you say elegant?"

"Yes. All our photographs are elegant. The brochure says so."

Q walked into the room and gave John a hug. "How was Millie?"

"Fine," said John.

"I heard," she said and walked back into the kitchen.

John sat down in the lone living room chair and looked at Arne. "How much vacation time can you get this summer?"

"Couple of weeks. Why?"

"Your alma mater will be announcing a grant for someone to photograph a few New England towns along the Canadian border. The photos will be published in a book and displayed at the East Side Gallery. The award will be $1,000 plus expenses."

"Nice. I'm sure there will be some competition for that one."

"It'll narrow down because you have to be a graduate of the college with experience in landscape photography. When you apply tell them about your work and suggest they expand the project to include a couple of sister towns across the border. This will add a strong human-interest element and create a Canadian market for the book."

"Great idea. And what will you be getting out of this?"

"I might be able to make an offer on the Blue Heron Press."

"Not bad. Then I can sell you my photographs."

"Stuffed mushrooms in the kitchen," said Q.

John opened the bottle of red, and for the next hour discussed the project. Arne suggested Q come along to talk with the townspeople, which she could do in English and French. John said he would drive his Bel Air because the trunk was large enough to hold their suitcases and Arne's camera equipment.

Three weeks later, the college posted the RFP. Arne filled it out and it was sent to the Blue Heron. The owner liked the idea of going across the border. Providence Arts College announced the grant recipient during a luncheon at the East Side Photo Lab gallery. The press was invited, and the next day the Journal carried a photo of the Blue Heron owner, the Photo Lab owners, Dr. Eldridge and Arne holding one of his cameras. No project had ever received a greater sendoff.

By mid-June, the towns were selected. Both boys trimmed their hair to create a look separate from the growing number of "hippies" who were becoming associated with illegal substances.

The three of them packed the Chevy early Saturday morning, and by 5 pm that afternoon were deep into New Hampshire territory driving along a secondary highway into the first town they would photograph, Marsden Mills. John continued driving until they reached the well-trimmed town square where the freshly painted town hall and Congregational Church faced off sixty yards apart across a freshly mowed lawn. Several small businesses fronted the square on two adjacent streets, which provided ample head-on parking.

They surveyed the area for buildings and angles that would provide vivid images, then expanded their walk beyond the square until they found the library, fire and police department, and elementary school. Arne noted the sun's location and decided to photograph each site in the morning and late afternoon. After receiving directions to the cemetery, they spent an hour surveying the headstones and writing down the older family names. Q used her 35mm Leica camera to photograph some of the older carvings. The advantage of a Leica, was the shutter made barely a whisper when a picture was taken. She liked the silence and was sure that those around her did as well.

They finished their preliminary work and drove to the motel outside of town to check in. John called the librarian, Helen Waters, to let her know they had arrived. She invited them to the church supper, that included strawberry shortcake.

Eager to get started, Arne placed his tripod in the center of the square, attached his camera, measured the light on the selected targets and bracketed his shots. When he finished, they photographed the library and firehouse. One of the young volunteer firemen came out to ask what they were doing. Arne explained the project with his usual enthusiasm, but the young boy couldn't keep his eyes off Q.

"I don't know who would buy that book around here?" he said, as if expecting them to be going door-to-door with order forms.

"Going to the church supper?" asked Q.

"Might be going with my friends."

"See you there," she said, giving him a wink.

At the supper, they met the librarian and were introduced to almost everyone in town assuring they would not escape notice during the next two days. Arne set up a time to photograph the mayor. After filling their plates with an assortment of home cooking, they sat down with Helen Waters and her husband who was fourth generation.

In most small towns, libraries are receptacles of old documents, official and unofficial, accurately written or layered with opinion piled into cardboard boxes collecting dust beneath a stairwell or locked inside a basement closet somewhere and the only one who knows where these riches lie is the librarian.

They learned that Marsden Mills was incorporated less than 150 years ago. Before that time the loggers and storekeepers didn't need anyone telling them what they couldn't do. John asked where they could find the historical plaque and was told it was at the north end of the highway to remind the Canadians they had roamed too far.

Q asked about family relations in the area.

"Most families chose which side of the border to set down their roots years ago, and very few have strayed." Said the librarian.

"Sometimes they forget," said Mr. Waters.

"Well," said his wife, "come spring, the grass always looks greener on the other side."

"There is a book in the library you can buy for eight bucks that'll give you the history of this place. Well written, too," said Mr. Waters.

Monday dawned with the sweetness of fragrant air filtered through woodlands and over fields of wildflowers surrounding the town. Arne took his photos including the town plaque, visited the library to buy the book for eight dollars, and photographed the mayor sitting behind his desk in the town hall. The next day they took the Chevy out into the countryside to photograph the hillsides, dairy herds with bowed heads, and any structure with a unique or contrasting configuration. John stopped by the library to say thank you and promised Helen they would send her a copy of the book when it was published.

"By the way, how far back do your husband's ancestors go?"

"To the fur traders," she said.

"So, his ancestors are Canadian?"

"Don't put that in your book." she said.

"I won't. Thanks again."

"Remember," she said, "there were no borders back then, and to some, there's none now. Have a pleasant trip."

They packed the car and headed southwest for two hours then North for another thirty to Galeford, a town on the New Hampshire-Vermont and Canadian line. It was easy to imagine the forefathers' frustration when they learned that their farms not only spread over two state lines but over two countries as well.

Galeford was smaller than Marsden Mills, but the town center had a hundred yards of sloping lawn pinioned by three large Victorian stone buildings with nothing else in view except the steeple of a church peeking through the top branches of the oak, maple and birch trees that hid everything below.

John parked his car next to a newer model of his Bel Air and a Ford truck. They proceeded up the steps and through the massive front door. They found the mayor and introduced themselves. They asked about the librarian and were told she works part-time in the school and could be found there. They were also told that all town activities took place at the fire station where there was room enough for everybody to sit down, speak up, or shut up, depending upon which was required at the time.

Arne pulled out his equipment to photograph the dark red stone buildings. John and Q took to the back roads searching for the school and the fire station, and then continued to find homes at the end of long driveways and farms with large stands of trees followed by and one hill after another that seemed to spill into Canada, unless they had been betrayed by their sense of direction.

By positioning his tripod on top of a two-foot-high berm, Arne could capture the entire sloping field and the three stone buildings. As he was preparing for his second shot, a large yellow tractor-trailer with a brown stripe and brown fenders came creeping around the corner. He waited until it was centered between the buildings and took the shot as a truck continued up the road. He jotted down the company name on the door and noted that it was a Kenworth tractor with the distinctive emblem of a swan facing forward on the hood.

That evening they met with the librarian and a few townspeople at the fire station for a group photo. The folks explained the town history and the wealthy family that built the three buildings in 1857 as a gift to the residents. The door opened and a woman with two children walked in to join her husband. Q asked if they would be willing to have a family picture taken. She learned that this was the Morse family, and the woman's husband Tom, was a trucker. When Arne heard this, he described the truck he saw in town and asked if that was his.

"It was mine. I saw you taking pictures when I went by," he said.

Arne spent two days photographing the farms and stone walls. The entire town rested on the side of a small mountain, which meant you drove either up or down to get where you were going.

They left the next morning for their first cross-border town. At the Port of Entry, they explained they were going to Milleau to photograph the town's historical buildings for a book. After inspecting Arne's equipment and contract documents, they were waved through to begin their Canadian trip on a two-lane highway that meandered twenty-five miles northwest and then ten miles in an easterly direction until reaching a small lake fed by a river that began thirty miles farther north. Milleau did not sit on the border but was as close as most small Canadian towns would get. While the American villages seemed to encroach on Canadian soil, the Canadian towns kept their distance.

The town was attractive but simple. There was no town square or other "wasted" space. It was simple in nature and built for ease of access by those who lived there. You drove in and you drove out without fuss or fanfare. That it was two-hundred years old and still standing as originally conceived, gave weight to the founders' foresight. One building housed all service departments, and the town library also functioned as the student's school library. Why buy two books when one would do.

While Arne worked with his camera, John and Q searched the cemetery headstones for names that would match up with any they had found south of the border. Before they left, John read the name of a woman and child who died on the same day in 1955.

That evening they had dinner with the two members of the governing Council. The Blue Heron Press picked up the tab. They discussed the local history and learned the first structure built was a trading post on the river where the French and Indians could meet and trade. The town only incorporated after the Mounted Police told them they would have to begin providing their own protection. John asked if any of the people had relatives across the border. They were told a couple of brothers with rigs lived below because it was closer to work, but that was all they knew of.

"In the cemetery we found a headstone with the name of a woman and a child who died the same day. Know what happened?" John asked.

"That was a while back" said one of the men, after which the conversation stopped.

To change the subject, Q asked what it was like to live there in the winter. "Do you get a lot of snow?"

"About as much as the next town," said the clerk.

They spoke more of the area and the families who had lived there the longest. After thanking the council members for their help, they paid the bill and headed back to the motel.

"Want to sample the local wildlife?" asked John. "There is a roadhouse ten minutes north."

"Shouldn't be too wild on a Tuesday." said Q.

They killed time rummaging through the local stores, then continued north until they found a barely lit parking lot and building that, from the outside, hadn't changed its appearance much since it housed hay and livestock. Other than the two men playing pool, they were the only customers. The bartender stood at least six feet tall. He had broad shoulders and hair just touching his ears.

"Three drafts," said Arne.

"Canadian or American?"

"Canadian," said Arne. He looked at John and Q. "When in Rome."

The beers came, and Arne handed him a twenty.

"We were hoping to find someone we could talk to about the town's history," said John.

"Ask them." said the bartender nodding toward the pool players.

John walked over to the men wearing construction boots, jeans and heavy cotton shirts. He approached the one not huddled over the table lining up his shot and said, "When you're through we'd like to buy you a beer."

"You play?"

"Not my game," said John, "but thanks."

Ten minutes later, the pool players joined them at a table. John motioned for more beer. Arne completed the introductions, explained their project, and asked if there were any families living in Milleau with relatives in Galeford. They didn't know of any.

John reached into his shirt pocket and pulled out a piece of paper. "Know anything about Amelia Betancourt Darnell?"

"Yeah," said one of the men, a bit harshly. "Amelia was married to Derek Darnell who got three years for burning down the hardware store."

"What happened to Amelia?"

"While everyone was at the store putting out the fire someone burned down their house. The next day they found Amelia and her daughter in the ashes."

"My God!" said Arne. "He did that?"

"Not according to the law. They only got evidence he burned down the store. He got three years for arson, and she and the baby got buried in the cemetery."

The other pool player leaned over the table and said, "Sure beats getting life for murder, don't it."

"Four years ago. So, he's out?"

"Yep."

"Is he around here?" asked John.

"Last I heard, was in Stanstead."

"Our next stop," said Q.

"You won't see him. He keeps out of sight. I wouldn't go looking for him neither; he's a mean son-of-a-bitch."

One of the players stood up. "Anyone for pool?"

"One game," said Q.

He racked the balls and told her she could start.

"Straight pool, nothing fancy," she said.

Q took a cue stick off the wall, rubbed the end with chalk, split the rack and ran every ball. She returned the stick and said: "Sorry."

The other player walked over to his buddy. "You got taken."

"She can take me anytime," he said with a grin.

Next morning Arne went out at sunrise for more pictures, then they packed up and drove sixty miles through the Canadian forests and farmland to their next town. Stanstead was larger than Milleau and bisected by a major highway that was busy during the day with trucks on their way to Montréal or over to Quebec.

The original highway was a narrow two-lane road packed with gravel and later oiled. The town developed on both sides continuing as far north as necessary with every building designed to remain forever where it had been set down. Thirty-five years later they were told the highway would be widened, and paved, so they jacked up every structure in use and moved them back two hundred feet onto new foundations.

By mid-afternoon, they had checked into the Byway Motel which had an attached restaurant and lounge. Arne was not excited about the photo opportunities. They visited the town hall to introduce themselves and were invited in for coffee. They spent an hour discussing the town's history and its relationship with Appeasement Village just south of the border, which would be the last town covered for the book. Arne said they would work out the locations to photograph the next day.

Ten miles out of town, they found a large barn converted into a restaurant. They were promptly seated and a two minutes later a waitress was at their table.

"You Americans?" she asked.

"How can you tell?" said Q.

The waitress smiled.

Arnie explained they were in Stanstead to photograph the historical buildings. "Any recommendations?"

The waitress thought for a moment, then said: "Any of those specials on the menu is good."

A short while later, the sound of sirens interrupted their meal. Three fire trucks raced past the restaurant disappearing down the main road. Ten minutes later they heard an explosion and looked over to see an exterior wall of the restaurant on fire burning through from the outside. Customers left their tables and rushed to the front door. John, Arne and Q walked back to where they were parked and noticed the car next to his had its windows smashed and the tires were flat.

A woman came toward them and screamed. "My car! Look at my car. That son of a bitch destroyed my car."

John recognized her as the waitress who served them. "Who did this?"

"My ex-boyfriend, that's who."

The flames had escaped through the roof of the building and were shooting into the sky. The heat of the fire became overwhelming.

"Where are the fire trucks?" said Arne.

The waitress turned to them. "At the other fire. I knew it was him who did this."

Q grabbed her arm. "Was your boyfriend Derek Darnell?"

"He was until I threw him out last week," she said. "Look at my car. Now I can't go anywhere."

Q held on to her arm. "Look around. Do you see him?"

"No," she said.

Q opened the car door. "Get in the back and sit on the floor," Q pushed her inside. "Let's get out of here," she said to John.

Once they were on the highway, Q told the waitress it was safe to sit up and asked for directions to her apartment. They drove through a neighborhood of two and three family homes. It wasn't long before he could smell the smoke and see the reflections of the fire engines' flashing lights.

"He burned my apartment!" she cried.

John drove the car around to the back of the building to look at the damage.

"He's gonna find me," said the waitress in fear.

"let's get back to the motel," said John.. While pulling into the parking lot, they saw a large yellow tractor-trailer parked off to the side next to a sign that read *Camions Bienvenue* A man and a young woman walked out of the motel room.

"Isn't that Tom Morse from Milleau?"

"Yeah," said John. "Don't look." He parked the car and sat for a minute to let them walk by.

Q took the waitress to her room and locked the door. She told the waitress to wash up in the bathroom and put on one of her shirts.

"I don't know what I'm going to do," said the waitress. "With my car gone I can't go anywhere."

"Where's your family?"

"I got a sister in Quebec," she said.

"Then go there."

"How? My car is destroyed."

"You're right. Let's go next door."

They left their room and went in to see John and Arne, where she laid out the problem, which was that they couldn't be in Québec and Stanstead at the same time.

"Trucks go there every day," said John.

"I wonder where Morse is headed?" said Arne.

"Far enough from his wife so he won't get caught with his girlfriend," said Q.

John looked at the waitress. "What do you wanna do?"

"Find a decent man to marry and settle down."

"Don't we all." said Q. She stood up and walked toward the door. "John, let's go talk to Morse and see where he's headed. I'll bring my camera." She looked at the waitress and Arne. "We'll be right back."

They walked into the lounge and found Morse and the young girl sitting next to each other in a booth holding hands. The drinks rested on the table. Q walked over, snapped a photo and slid into the booth across from them.

"Nice to see you again. We have a question."

Morse's ruddy complexion disappeared when the blood drained from his face. He dropped his girlfriend's hand and moved away. Before he could say a word, Q asked where he was delivering his next load. As soon as the words left her mouth she almost laughed. "I'm referring to your truck."

Morse dropped his shoulders and looked at the table. "Montréal."

Q stood up and looked at the girlfriend. "I'm going to the lady's room. Why don't you join me?"

She nodded meekly.

Morse moved out of her way. Once inside, Q noticed that the girl had a slight build and was modestly dressed. She certainly wasn't a hooker.

"How long have you known Tom?"

"For a while," she said.

"So, what are your plans?"

"He's pretty busy. He comes by when he can."

Q saw a naïve woman hoping to find someone help her escape from a small town and maybe more.

"What does he do?" she asked.

The young girl spoke innocently and painfully. "Drives his truck all over," she said.

"Suppose we drive down to Milleau where you can meet his wife and two children."

"What are you talking about?"

Q placed a photo in front of her.

The girl looked at it and started to cry.

"Don't think too much about it," said Q. "I'm going back to talk to Morse. Why don't you stay in here until you're ready to leave." She left the young girl with both hands gripping the wash-basin counter looking at the reflection of a distraught and deceived woman.

Q returned to the booth. "Your girlfriend may be tied up for a while and we have other business. Mr. Morse, we have a friend who is being stalked by her boyfriend and needs a ride to Québec." Q took out the piece of paper with the address and handed it to him. "I know you have to go to Montréal, so consider Québec a side trip."

"Side trip!" He said," Hell, I'd lose a day of work and a hundred in fuel. I can't afford that."

She glared at him. "You've already lost the day stopping here so I don't think your schedule is that tight and I can't imagine how much money you'd lose if your wife and children knew you've been seeing another woman."

"You bitch!"

John leaned forward to protect Q. "Mr. Morse, the loss of one day to save your marriage is a small price to pay."

"And if I say yes? What then?"

"We'll have her here at seven tomorrow morning. You drive to Québec and drop her off at the address we give you. She calls to let us know she arrived, and you'll never hear from us again." John held out his hand, "Deal?"

"She is a nice girl. You'll enjoy the ride," said Q.

They left the booth and returned to the motel room. Q told the waitress she'd be at her sister's house tomorrow in time for dinner.

The next morning Arne began photographing the town while the waitress climbed up into the passenger seat of the big yellow rig and admired the view. She waved goodbye to Q and gave the driver a sweet smile.

Later that day, John and Q met with department heads in the town hall conference room for their official photo. They mentioned they had been in the restaurant last night that burned down.

"Firebombed," said the fire chief.

"Know who did it?" asked Arne.

"We know," said the chief. "They picked him up early this morning. He was on the highway walking toward the motel with a loaded gun."

A trickle of sweat rolled down John's neck at the thought of Darnell showing up at his motel door with a gun in his hand.

"What will happen to him," he asked.

"Burning down two buildings will put him back in prison, carrying a gun while on parole will add a few more years. and resisting arrest and threatening an officer with a gun will keep him behind bars well into his golden years."

"He threatened an officer with his gun?"

"Anytime we see a gun, we feel threatened," he smiled.

Arne put his camera equipment away, and they shook hands. "We'll be taking a few more pictures this afternoon before we leave.

By the way, I want to get an oil change and heard Darcy's is a good place. Can you tell me how to get there?"

That afternoon John brought his car over to the Garage. They told him to leave it, and they would get it done before closing. One of the mechanics gave him a ride back to the motel.

They spent the afternoon visiting some of the shops and enjoying lunch. By late afternoon the phone rang in John's motel room. It was the waitress telling John she was in Québec and to thank everyone for her.

The mechanic arrived to drive John to the shop to pick up his car. He paid his bill and returned to town. John suggested they pack up and leave for Appeasement Village rather than stay over another night. No one objected to leaving Stanstead behind. Two hours later they were across the border seated at a restaurant a mile from their destination.

Appeasement Village was founded in 1701 as a conciliatory gesture between two quarrelsome brothers with vicious wives who, given the chance, would have shot each other without a second thought. Their houses were built at the opposite ends of the town. The village never grew beyond its nineteenth-century size, and there was no reason to live there other than a pristine lake and unspoiled countryside.

The team followed the same procedure that worked so well in the previous towns. The older wooden structures would photograph beautifully, the retired population were willing to take a group picture, and most important, they found the iconic covered bridge built across a stream, that is essential to every book about New England. After spending two days in this picture-perfect town, they turned south, hoping to reach Concord by nightfall.

"So," said Arne to John, "now that the trip is over, are you really gonna buy the Blue Heron Press?"

"We'll have to see," said John.

Two days later, on a warm August morning, John eased his 235 cubic-inch inline-6 five-year old 54 Chevy Bel Air Sports Coupe onto the gravel parking lot fronting Pritchard's garage for an oil change, grease-job, and a fluid check. There was only one other car ahead of him.

Once inside the garage, two men with tools opened the front doors, carefully unscrewed the inside panels, and removed the sealed containers of drugs, which they placed in the trunk of the waiting car.

Thompson told John that after he delivered the merchandise, he would return with his share of the money, which would be enough to make an offer on his father's business. He drove out of the garage across the gravel parking lot, lit a joint, inhaled deeply, and turned onto the highway to drive out of town.

John waited while they finished the work on his Bell Air, paid the bill, and backed out of the parking lot onto route 1A. He drove no more than five miles when he reached the long bend in the road. Slowing down, he saw the flashing red lights of fire engines, police cars and a rescue truck at the gas station. A car, instead of negotiating the long curve, continued in a straight line into an island of gas pumps. Thankfully, there were no flames.

John pulled off the road and left his car. After walking around the fire engine, he recognized Thompson's car. Upon impact, the hood and trunk snapped open. Thompson had been thrown into the windshield and then back into the front seat and was now pinned by the steering wheel. The firemen's' first priority was to foam the area and shut off the fuel to the pumps. The police were inspecting the vehicle, and it was a tossup as to whether the body, or bags of drugs would be removed from the car first.

Though John was greatly relieved that he would no longer have to be involved with Thompson, he could not dismiss his anger at the dead man behind the wheel for screwing up his chance to buy the Blue Heron Press. *What a jerk*, he thought.

Later that afternoon, while sitting on his front porch looking between the two houses, across the parking lot to the harbor beyond with the sailboats moored on both sides of the channel and a steady stream of actors walking across his personal proscenium arch, John could not decide whether his fortune was good or bad, or whether all along, his chances for one or the other were never more than the flip of a coin, and if that was the case, should another opportunity of such magnitude cross his path again, he would leave the coin in his pocket, and call it a day.

Rhode Island 1982

Seventy-Five Cents
on the Dollar

Bobby is eighty-nine years old and beginning to have doubts about how much longer he will be able to take his morning walks, jump up and down on his trampoline, row his 1969 wooden rowing machine and play tennis. Me too, Bobby. Me too.

I turned seventy-five last November having lived in various circumstances for three-quarters of a century. That's seventy-five cents on the dollar. To describe those years would be difficult. I don't have the energy or the interest, and I don't know anyone that concerned. I will tell you though, I am surprised to have lived this long and cringe at the memories of death's lost opportunities.

At the age of ten I rode my bike hell-bent across a highway without looking left or right. I went into shock the second I realized my mistake and don't remember how I reached the other side without being hit or causing an accident. One summer, I came close to drowning when stomach cramps doubled me up fifty yards off shore. There were others. Only the hand of retribution has allowed me to live this long because my punishment is not being allowed to forget the past.

Longevity involves the storage and retrieval of memories, including those of careless mistakes and thoughtless decisions that benefited no one. Longevity is bearing witness to the dying of people and pets, woods stripped naked for housing, and the ocean I loved as a boy becoming polluted and starved for oxygen. Longevity is attesting to a world that is cluttered with inarticulate leadership expressing ineffective views, regression, and futility. The list goes on.

Other than the deterioration of our planet, insufferable mankind and those damn memories, living long is not bad. One benefit to remaining above ground is being able to close your eyes and fall asleep any afternoon without being chastised, at least not in your presence. The rewards of napping are second only to receiving a radiant smile and heartfelt care. When you are tired, bliss is a warm blanket and a good book.

Of course, not everyone enjoys reading, including my friend Harry Winston. No, not the wealthy jeweler who donated the Hope Diamond to the Smithsonian the year I graduated from high school. My friend is the other Harry. I did tell him though, the next time around, he should get into precious stones.

Harry watches sports on television under a warm blanket accompanied, not by a book, but by his adoring wife whom he cherishes even more. So, I was surprised when he said to me he knew a "great" nursing home where we could "raise hell together." This sounded like fun until I considered the energy needed to "raise hell" and how little I would have when that time came. In the event, however, there was the slightest chance of raising hell, on the third Thursday in July, Harry and I took a ride to our future home.

"You're gonna love it," he said." You should see the nurses."

"Registered?" I asked, knowing the thin profit margin of a business that required federal funds to make payroll.

"Assistants," he said. "They're even better."

Better? How? I wondered. I don't know, maybe he was right. This was new to me. We drove into a gravel parking lot of a recently painted large home from the past century fronted by a wide porch with a deep slanting roof supported by eight pillars.

"This must have been something in its day," I said.

"Wait'll you see inside. They've got a plaque of the owner."

"What's his name?"

Harry tilted his head, wondering why I'd ask him such a question, when the answer was displayed on a wall inside the building. Then he remembered. "The guy's named was Brennan."

"That guy?" I said, pointing to the sign on the lawn that read "Brennan Nursing Home."

"Yea, that's the guy, Patrick Brennan. Made his money selling booze,"

I laughed because that was a name I knew. "Yes, he did. He sold lots of booze."

As I remembered the story, Patrick Brennan was a wholesale liquor salesman in the late 1800s. He moved north a year after his friend, John Gordon, part owner of an Irish bar in the city of Cranston, became the prime suspect in the death of Amasa Sprague, a textile factory owner. Amasa, a man of great strength, was beaten to death on New Year's Eve in 1843 while walking from his mansion to his farm.

Some of his Irish mill workers ate lunch in Gordon's bar and returned to work with more than one drink under their belt. This made Amasa angry and he berated them in front of the other men. He tried in vain through legislation to close the bars during the day. His dislike for the Irish was well known even though they supplied cheap labor for his mill. So, it was not unreasonable to suspect that one or more of those workers murdered Amasa, but instead, the police arrested the man who owned the bar, John Gordon. And for good measure they arrested his two brothers, his mother and impounded his dog. This is all true. At the urging of Judge Job Durfee, who told the jurors to give greater weight to the Yankee witnesses than the Irish, twelve Englishmen decided John Gordon, a "filthy Irishman" from "Monkeytown," as Knightsville was scurrilously labeled at the time, had to be guilty.

Gordon wasn't guilty of murder, but he was guilty of being a dirty Irish-Catholic immigrant, and that was enough for the English to hang any one of them. Gordon was the last man in Rhode Island to receive the death penalty.

After seeing how easy it was for an Irishman to be convicted of a crime he did not commit, Patrick Brennan, the immigrant Irish wholesaler who stocked the Irish bars, moved his Irish business north to be among the French Canadians living in Woonsocket. Brennan did not add water to his liquor or charge more than necessary to make an honest profit. He became a respected businessman and prosperity followed. Mr. Brennan built a home on five acres of land overlooking Harrisville Pond.

Seven years after learning they hanged an innocent man, the Rhode Island General Assembly abolished the death penalty, but by then Brennan had no reason to move back to "Monkeytown." He and his family lived on the estate he had built until everyone had passed away or moved on. His surviving niece donated the home to the Sisters of Saint Francis for the care of aging parishioners, just before moving to California with John Martin Feeney, a talented Irishman from Cape Elizabeth, Maine.

*

After Henry VIII evicted the Pope in 1534 from English soil, the English nobility believed they would never have to abide the likes of those Catholics again and certainly not across the sea where they had recently colonized a new world on the backs of savages. It didn't work out. Why God continued to punish them so, they did not know. But He did.

First, one and a half million Irish-Catholics followed them across that same sea for food and work, but found instead, continued misery under the thumb of the land-owning Protestant "Yankee" mill owners with ties to the founding fathers they would never let you forget. Fifty years later, a second wave of immigrants came ashore, four-million Italian-Catholics also looking for a better place to live. No one warned these wine-making foodies that their presence would give the Irish a boost up the social ladder, or that the Irish would be hired by the Yankees to keep the Italians in their place. Thousands of burley, young Irishmen were given a night stick, a blue jacket and a badge they attached to where most people think the human heart is located. It isn't.

The Irish treated the Italians the same way the Protestants had treated them. The Irish learned fast, and they had the right of first in. The Italians did not accept this indignity and created their own police force to protect themselves from the Irish, the Yankees, and from each other. Their police force was called the Mafia.

*

I asked Harry, "How did you find out about this nursing home?"

"Bobby told me."

"Bobby? Our Bobby?"

"Yeah, our Bobby. How many Bobby's you know?" Harry had the habit of looking you right in the eye when he answered a question that was a waste of his time.

Bobby played tennis with us, us being a small group of older men capable of swinging a racket but less capable of moving around the court as we had years earlier. His birth name was Roberto Antonio da Vinci, but no one called him Roberto since he was born in America, thanks to his Italian Catholic immigrant parents who lived under the thumb of the Irish, the mill owners and the church in that order. Instead, everyone called him Bobby.

When we play tennis with someone new, we call them by their first name. We don't think about last names unless we're looking for

179

someone in the obituary column. Often enough, first names max out our short-term memory, anyway, and at our age everything is short term. What we care about, is how well they play. If they play below our level, they disrupt the game. If they play above our level, they also disrupt the game. Either way, it doesn't work out.

When Bobby did tell me his full name, *Roberto Antonio da Vinci*, I asked if he were related to Leonardo da Vinci. He said he didn't know.

"Are you kidding?" I said. "You never looked to see if you were related to Leonardo da Vinci? You know who I'm talking about, right?"

Bobby laughed and asked how it would make any difference. I said I didn't know. Then he said, "Well, I couldn't be related, because Leonardo didn't have any children."

So, after all that, Bobby did know whether or not he was related to Leonardo da Vinci, and of course, he wasn't.

Walking toward the porch of the Brennan Nursing Home, I asked Harry, "How does Bobby know about this place?"

"His wife's here."

"His wife's here? I didn't know that. How long?"

"Three years."

I thought about that. "So, your plan is for us to move in with another man's wife?"

"They keep the women in another wing."

"Then how do we raise hell?" I think I got him on that one because he didn't have an answer.

Before we reached the steps, Bobby came through the front door and stood on the porch that had been called a veranda when he was a young boy. He didn't notice us until Harry yelled his name. Bobby was twelve years older than Harry, but without missing a beat he recognized us off the court and began to laugh.

"What are you doing here?" he said.

"Harry wants us to move in and raise hell," I offered.

Bobby laughed again, this time at the futility of Harry's proposition, but told Harry it was a good idea anyway. He said the place needed shaking up. "I come here to visit my wife," he said. He didn't tell us he planned to move in. He had already met with the administrator to sign the "get-in" papers. Bobby would spend his last summer in the house he and his wife had lived in for fifty-seven years then turn it over to his children. Before the snow flew in November, he expected to be inside the nursing home under a warm blanket.

Bobby said he would show us around. Harry said he knew his way around and didn't need Bobby. They looked at each other for a while until Bobby shook his head. "You don't know anything about this place," he said. "I come here every day, and I know everything."

Harry and Bobby had been playing tennis and squabbling for twenty years. Bobby looked at me and said: "He knows I know more than he does. He just won't admit it."

Bobby did know more than Harry, because his life came to pass within the depths of humanity, while Harry's experienced life at arm's length. This was not Harry's fault; his life just happened that way.

Harry is eighty cents on the dollar. He joined the air force on June 12, 1953, the day after high-school graduation. He wanted to bomb the hell out of the North Koreans and also the Chinese who were sneaking over the border to help. The Air Force trained him to become a B29 Super fortress radio operator. On July 22nd, Harry flew west over the Pacific Ocean to the 98th Bombardment Squadron in South Korea. One week later, General William Harrison signed the Armistice agreement. It was the first time America signed a treaty without winning a war. The "war" started and ended at the same spot, the 38th Parallel. It was a tie.

A sergeant from staff headquarters assigned Harry to a B29 rebuilt from spare parts. The job of this relic was to drop a half million tons of surplus bombs on a deserted village north of a treeless ridge. The plane carried a twenty-thousand-pound payload each trip. That was enough for twenty-five bombing runs. If the war had not ended, Harry would have earned a ribbon.

The Air Force didn't want to ship anything back to the States, so they bombed an empty village and surrounding countryside into ruble over and over again until the last deafening sound of exploding ordinance faded across the Bukhan River. All that remained of the half million tons of destructive force were fragments of aluminum casings scattered over one square mile of blackened earth, except for a few unauthorized locations the bombardier targeted through his Norden bombsight when he became bored.

Although the flash of the explosions could be seen and heard for twenty miles, from his seat in the B29 facing a wall of transmitters, tuners, receivers, amplifiers and trailing wire, Harry never saw a thing outside the plane.

After the Korean War, Harry became a warehouse manager. Under his direction, the building expanded to the size of two football fields. Harry was a marvel. He moved thousands of boxes in and out every day with record efficiency, but he never saw the products in the stores or the customers who bought them. From his seat inside the four-story structure, stacked floor to ceiling with goods of every description. Harry never saw a thing outside the building.

Bobby fought in the Fifth Army's 88th Division all the way to Rome. On June 4th, 1944, the 88th entered the city. The next day thousands of grateful citizens swarmed into the streets to celebrate the victory and personally thank every soldier they saw. Bobby never forgot that moment. June 5th was the greatest day in his life. After the

Japanese surrendered, he was sent to Hiroshima with a team to inspect the damage. There was a lot.

Two months later, Bobby returned home to start a small grocery store. He helped his customers six days a week and communed with them on the seventh. Everyone loved him. Roberto Antonio "Bobby" da Vinci experienced the liberation of Rome every day of his life.

Bobby took us inside the nursing home where staff members greeted him warmly. He was the only man to visit his wife every day; a record, he pointed out, that would never be broken. Harry said hello to the staff but didn't receive the response he was looking for. It was probably too early to start raising hell.

"What'd you think of the nurses?" asked Harry.

"Assistants," I corrected. "By the time we get here, they'll be retired, and we'll be too old to remember."

Harry nudged my arm. "There'll be others."

He was right. Nursing homes will always be staffed by good-hearted women who like old people. But the thought of ogling legs in white stockings and bodies in white uniforms dampened my enthusiasm for raising hell, or what I thought Harry meant by raising hell. Harry never explained what he meant, and the notion of raising hell may have been as vague to him as it was to me.

Bobby began the tour on the first floor. He took us to the activity room, dining room, kitchen, meeting rooms and offices for the secretary, the director, and the head nurse. Patrick Brennan's estate was large, meticulously restored and repainted in original early American colors. Each room reflected 19th-century character with craftsmanship unavailable in new construction today. I was impressed.

I restored a Victorian house years ago and appreciated the effort and skill required for the Brennan estate. Coincidently, my Victorian had been converted to a nursing home before I bought it, and later a boarding house with rooms for single men. Rooms were partitioned to create additional bedrooms. Workmen installed drop ceilings to conserve heat, and in the style of the day, covered the horse-hair plaster with paneling. My first job was to tear out that paneling and remove two hundred white-dimpled ceiling tiles. Dumpsters were filled and hauled away.

Although my craftsmanship did not compare to the restoration of Patrick Brennan's home, when it came time to sell, the house caught the eye of a couple who loved the area, though to my dismay, I was sure they would disregard my restoration with alterations to fit their needs with one exception. On the back of the property, I built an eighty-foot-long stone retaining wall. This was my contribution to perpetuity. May the world never end.

*

We looked down the long hallway of an added wing with bedrooms on either side. "This wing is for the women," said Bobby. "My wife's room is down there. The wing upstairs is for men."

Bobby took us on the elevator to the second floor and then back down to the lobby.

I asked Bobby about the empty room on the men's floor.

"It won't be for long," he replied.

"Maybe that's your room, Harry?" I said.

The three of us stood outside on the veranda looking at stands of maple and pine, a green lawn, and the gravel parking lot full of cars with the sun glinting off their hoods, wishing we were back a hundred years.

Bobby looked over at Harry. "You want to come here? You've got a wife at home. Why do you want to come here?"

Harry looked him in the eye. "Why, you, don't want me here?" Harry had decided that this was the best nursing home around, and there was nothing anyone could say that would change his mind. He had felt the same way about the Air Force when he joined. He didn't know why, he just did. Like most of us, he couldn't explain his reasons, or his feelings, most of the time, and that was okay because to do so required more insight and energy then most of us possess.

Before they said another word, an antique faded dark-green-colored military car drove into the parking lot with an American flag flying from the front bumper stopping 30-feet from the porch.

James Patterson, age ninety-one, full of indifference and with a history of questionable judgment, needed professional care. He was a thirty-year military man who rose to the rank of sergeant more than once and was reluctant to retire. He later became a police officer in an unincorporated town along Highway 70, south of Sweetwater, Texas. With little to do, he drank heavily. Six months before today, Patterson's son, Randall, flew to Fort Worth, puddle jumped to Abilene then took a Trailways bus to the Pearl Motel. He grabbed his alcoholic father out of his motel room, put him in the back seat and drove across country to Blackstone, Massachusetts. He parked the WW2 relic in the garage and parked his father in a rehab center to dry out.

Sergeant James Patterson, in a return to family tradition, named his son, Randall, after his great-great- great-grandfather who died in an Indian raid with General George Custer during the battle of Greasy Grass in 1876, and his great-great-grandfather who died in the Spanish-American war tromping up San Juan heights with Colonel Teddy Roosevelt behind the buffalo soldiers in 1898, and his great-grandfather who died from a sniper's bullet meant for General Blackjack Pershing during the battle of Belleau Woods in WWI. All had been named Randall, and all died in one war, or another, in the presence of legendary soldiers, which is why his grandmother wrote "James" on her son's birth certificate so he wouldn't suffer the same fate. It worked. James Patterson did not die in combat and is alive today.

By the time Randall sat in the pilot's seat of a B29 in South Korea, the curse had worn off. He survived the "war" and lived long enough to deliver his father to the Brennan Nursing Home the day after rehab pronounced the old man sober.

Randall, with his wife next to him in the front seat, drove to the Brennan Nursing Home while his father sat in the back of his 1941 Pontiac Torpedo four-door sedan with a large white, five-pointed star on the front door and a flag holder bolted to the front bumper. The army had printed "U.S.A. 63025" on the hood to distinguish it from the hundreds they bought that year for their officers. The small American flag attached to the driver side bumper had flapped back and forth the entire trip and now stood at ease. During the ride, his father thought about the past, his childhood, his time served, and all that fate had delivered.

*

Robert Oppenheimer and his associates in Los Alamos built two atomic bombs. The first was Little Boy, a uranium projectile dropped on Hiroshima August 6th by the B29 Enola Gay, (named after the pilot's mother), and Fat Man, an implosion type bomb dropped on Nagasaki August 9th by the B29 Bockscar (named after Captain Bock), but flown, in a last-minute change, by Major Charles Sweeney.

The Japanese used 353 planes to bomb the Pearl Harbor Navy Base, while the United States defeated their entire nation with only two, a record never to be broken. And the reason they bombed Nagasaki, was the city of Kokura had clouded over preventing visual contact by the bombardier. Descendants of the families who lived in Kokura, are now living productive lives today thanks to the deteriorating weather of August 9th, 1945.

In the event either of these planes developed a mechanical problem, a third B29 waited on the tarmac with engines running smoothly, in the bright sunshine of that morning. If this backup plane had lifted off the runway over the white sands of Tinian Island, Sergeant James Patterson, first class radio operator, would have participated in dissolving either Nagasaki or Hiroshima. But facing a row of communication equipment during the flight, he would not have seen anything outside the plane, not even the most brilliant flash ever created by man.

Sergeant Patterson sat in the back of his beloved Pontiac Torpedo waiting for his daughter-in-law to open the rear door, which she did.

He stepped out wearing his flight jacket and faded air force cap. Spotting the veranda, he quick-stepped his way to the staircase leaving everyone behind. He marched up the three steps, turned to address his support staff, of which half had returned to the car, changed his mind, turned again, opened the nursing home door and disappeared inside. Patterson seemed unaware that three men stood next to him on the porch. It may have been that they were out of uniform.

"Who's that guy?" asked Harry.

"The guy who's going to live in the empty room," said Bobby.

Harry drove me home while I thought about something else.

When you're seventy-five-cents on the dollar, memories take up more time than shopping, and the price is higher. When I'm pushing a carriage between cans of soup and boxes of dry pasta, I try not to think about my past.

Harry parked his car next to the garage and walked inside the house to wait for his wife and daughter to return from grocery shopping. He called Bobby to ask if he could visit the home with him the next day. Bobby said anytime. Harry wondered out loud to Bobby how much longer he would be able to play tennis. Tennis is important no matter how old you are.

Bobby reminded me that good knees are necessary to play tennis and stay in shape. Without them, you can't move your legs. Moving your legs increases your heart rate, which in turn, burns calories. You must burn as many as you take in to keep the weight off, unless it is already there, then you have to burn more. Let me give you one of my favorite examples. A good beer is a wonder to behold, but there is a price to pay beyond the bar tab, getting rid of the extra calories. I use a treadmill. I can burn off 180 calories cruising at a twelve-minute mile for fifteen minutes or increase my pace to a 10.9 minute-mile and do the job in ten. But I couldn't use a treadmill without good knees, and I'd have to give up beer.

*

James Patterson hesitantly entered the room where he would spend the rest of his life. He looked in the closet, the bathroom, then out the window. He could see a few trees, a lightly traveled two-lane road, buildings in both directions, and people walking by who would never know he was there. He sat down in a soft-cushioned, blue-upholstered chair that he would use to entertain company and watch television. It was more comfortable than the chair back in his motel room and cleaner.

Randall filled the closet and the dresser drawers with everything his father owned, with one exception. He kept the 45-caliber handgun. Handguns are not allowed in nursing homes. I can understand why for two reasons, homicide and suicide. There may others I don't know of

A recently dried-out James Patterson with occasional memory loss, picked up his copy of *Fire of a Thousand Suns* written by Enola-Gay tail-gunner, Staff Sergeant George R. "Bob" Caron, and held it firmly in his lap. He didn't say a word. A nurse's assistant entered the room and introduced herself as Giselle. Randall said goodbye to his father, walked to the car, slid behind the wheel and turned the key.

He drove his father's Pontiac out of the parking lot onto the highway. The small American flag snapped back and forth leading the way. Randall's wife became bored and leaned against the driver's side door. She watched her husband drive the heavy sedan with both hands on the steering wheel and moved her left leg up onto the seat resting her foot across Randall's lap.

"How many officers do you think got lucky in this car during the war?" she asked.

*

Giselle placed James Patterson's book on his bed and coaxed him out of the upholstered chair. She walked him into the activity room to join three men sitting at a table with a deck of cards in front of them. The cards were not being played. Sometimes people ignore what is in front of them for no apparent reason. This was one of those times.

She encouraged all the men to spend more time together. It was a struggle. During her two years at the home, she noticed men socialize less than women. She might not know this, but men have too much to think about, and the days fly. Anthropologists discovered years ago that males like to be with others when they eat and drink or laugh. That's about it.

Patterson sat down at the table and introduced himself as the "wholesale slaughter man." The others looked up and smiled. "Glad to meet you, I'm John the meat packer," said one of the men who then looked to his right, "and this is Roland the mechanic." He pointed to the third man sitting at the table. "This is the other John. He's in sales too. So, what do you wholesale? I hope it's liquor because you can't get a drink around here for crap."
"I can't drink anymore. I dried out last week."

189

"None of us drink. I just wondered what you wholesaled."

"Wholesaled slaughter. Remember Enola Gay?"

No one at the table could think of anyone by that name.

Patterson recounted. "The plane, Enola Gay the plane."

"Hiroshima Enola Gay?"

"Hiroshima Enola Gay. I've got the book in my room with pictures," said Patterson.

"You in the book?"

"I was a radio man on the War Machine, but our plane never took off. The Japs surrendered before we could launch. But we were ready. Even had shirts made up said "Wholesale Slaughter Gang.""

"But you never launched?"

"Just sat there on the runway 'til they shipped us home."

*

Later that afternoon Bobby called me. He wanted to know how I was feeling. I told him fine. He wondered why I was at the nursing home with Harry. I said it was to give him support.

"You're not ready to go in?" he asked.

"No," I said.

"Good," he said back. "You're too young."

*

Harry's daughter drove into the driveway. His wife opened the passenger door and walked toward the house carrying a bag of groceries. His daughter walked next to her carrying two more. Harry's wife became dizzy, lost her balance, and fell to the ground. Her daughter knelt down to hold her. She loved her mother very much and cared deeply for her father. Harry called 911. This was not the first time she had fallen. Harry began to cry. It was time.

*

We learn when raising children, there comes an age after which our best intentions are deflected by the influence of their friends. They become members of an evolving assembly who dress alike, talk alike, and think out loud alike. Silently, they think differently, often with intensity and sometimes with devastating results, but when they are together, there is nothing you can do to stem the tide. We become acutely aware of our children's friends and try to understand their values, which we measure against our own, and what we believe is best for our children. Weighing and measuring our rock-bound principles against changing trends and natural growth is exhausting. You have to be prepared. You have to be fit.

Living in good health is the key to longevity. The key to good health is plenty of sleep, water and exercise. For example, once a day, I work through a twenty-minute routine learned in high school; jumping jacks, touching toes, push-ups, and sit ups, etc. If these exercises sound outdated to you, remember they were used to prepare twelve-million men for battle, which was enough to win two world wars. If those exercises were good enough for those men, they are good enough for me. I can finish my set in the time it would take me to drive to a health club. And just so you know, lack of coordination or second-rate athletic ability make no difference. It is movement, though sometimes flailing, that keeps you alive. With perseverance and effort, I may live for many years, or the blood clot in my leg could float up stream into my lungs causing my death at any time. I am no different than those who lived in Kokura or Nagasaki. Living long depends on circumstances, and that is all.

For Christmas, my daughter gave me the book, *Running Until you're 100*. The title brought me up short, not the running part, but the living until you are one-hundred part. Living another twenty-five will take a lot of work. The book gives older runners permission to combine running and walking to reach their mileage. I like that, but I'm not ready to walk. The author covers in detail how to train and provides charts on how to measure and increase pace and endurance.

My experience is this. If you want to run faster, run faster. If you want to run longer, run longer. Run until you're out of breath or feel your body falling apart. The trick is to know the difference between discomfort and injury. You push through the first and lay up on the second. My other suggestion is to stand up straight with your shoulders back when you run. Stand up straight with your shoulders back when you walk. And stand up straight with your shoulders back when you hang out. There is something else.

Change is important and role models are reminders of what we might yet become. Our first role model should be the physical properties that hold us together. These are the cells in our body. They regenerate and renew every day we are alive. We can do the same by trying out the productive and admirable traits of others, or what we would like to become. Here is how it works.

Bobby is a natural athlete with the balance, eye-hand coordination and core strength to play any sport well. More important, he plays for pleasure without the anxious need to win or wreak havoc. He is quick to remind you that the game is no fun if you're not having good, unless I got it backwards. He's role model number one. There is another tennis player in our group with an attitude so positive she loves every shot no matter where it goes and loves every game no matter who wins. She's role model number two. See how it works? We're not looking to become someone else, just selecting the trait we want to try on. Some may counter with, I just want to be myself, but the fact is, everything you are is based on what you learned from others since the day you were born. You are already a compilation of everyone you have met, so don't stop growing just yet. And next, there is that complicated issue of reasonable and proper nourishment.

If you plan your meals around food that grows above the earth and below the sea, and drink lots of water, you are better off. Salt, sugar, soda and processed foods reduce the quality of life and your life span. Millions of Americans do not learn this until they are diagnosed with diabetes. Then they follow the above restrictions faithfully. They also supplement their diet with insulin and skin punctures, which increases the profits of the pharmaceuticals by billions of dollars.

I know what you're thinking. You can eat anything in moderation. Our bodies can handle an occasional chip, a can of soda, fried pork, Slim Jim and a Twinkie. You're right. You can even take rat poison in moderation. I take 2.5 mg. every night prescribed by my doctor then wait around for six hours to see if I wake up in the morning.

Warfarin sodium, first used as rat poison, is the miracle drug. When chemists studied how this coagulation inhibitor in the white crystalline powder so effectively eliminated rodents, they found it thinned the blood right out through their little pores. The rats died but never had a blood clot. Eureka! Anything that works for rats, works for man, there being little difference between the two. The miracle drug created another billion-dollar windfall for you know who. Every American with a blood clot or coming out of surgery is prescribed rat poison in one form or another.

*

After the Fifth Army liberated the Eternal City, Captain Hollister assigned Bobby's platoon the job of setting up housing for the command staff while the rest of the 88th took the fight to Berlin. In a second-level basement of a large home recently occupied by a

German colonel and his mistress, Bobby discovered a wine cellar stocked floor to ceiling. Two blocks west, he created a piazza in a bombed-out church. His men set up tables and chairs for the citizens, so they could sit down and catch their breath. He supplied the bakery shops with flour, yeast, and sugar so the bakers could go back to work. They brought bread and pastry to the citizens sitting in the chairs. Others came with pasta and soup. Bobby supplied the wine and musicians brought their instruments to entertain.

When Bobby returned home to run his grocery store, he used the basement to make wine and share the space with others. They hosted block parties on warm summer nights. Some neighbors brought bread and pastry and others brought pasta and soup. Bobby supplied the wine, and musicians brought their instruments to entertain.

*

Harry called 911 when his wife fell. The EMTs brought her to the hospital emergency room. The staff did not have the training to treat her condition and sent her to a larger hospital twelve miles away. Before the ambulance returned to the highway, the doctor typed in a diagnosis that only the insurance company would see. A month later the hospital would be reimbursed for an event long forgotten and a service never provided.

Harry's wife rested in a hospital bed for tests and observation. They assessed her memory and physical balance. Memory loss is a predictor of longevity as sure as the lines on the palm of your hand, and balance is a predictor of whether that longevity will be spent standing up or sitting down for the rest of your life.

Harry went back to the Brennan Nursing Home with Bobby. While Bobby sat with his wife in the activity room, Harry talked to the administrator. The social worker told Harry she would contact the hospital to begin arrangements. Hospital and nursing home social workers are on a first-name basis. Inquiries, arrangements, and transfers from one facility to the other, no matter how tragic and unsettling, take place frequently and flow smoothly along a well-worn path with measured progress and systematic inevitability.

Harry returned to the activity room, but instead of sitting with Bobby and his wife, sat at a table with four men waiting for time to pass. "Mind if I join you?" he asked.

"You here to see Wholesale?"

"Who's Wholesale?"

"Me," said James Patterson.

The first man continued. "He got dropped off last week and hasn't had a visitor yet. He hasn't figured out this ain't a destination resort. "

Harry laughed. "It's pretty nice in here, though." He looked across the room toward Bobby and his wife. "See those two over there. He comes here every day to see his wife."

"Bobby. Yeah, we know him. Hell-of-a-guy. They're love birds, those two."

Harry looked at Wholesale and commented on his Air Force flight jacket. Patterson told him about Enola Gay and how he had been a radio man in a brand-new B29 made special from the States but sat on the runway and never got to drop the bomb. Harry told Patterson how he flew in an old beat-up B29 as a radio operator in Korea.

"Maybe we were on the same plane, in different wars," he said.

Patterson sat up and showed some interest. "My God, wouldn't that be something? Where'd you fly?"

"South Korea in the Eighty-Ninth."

"Eighty-Ninth? My son flew in the Eighty-Ninth. He was a pilot."

"We had hundreds. By the end of the war, we had more planes, pilots, and bombs than we knew what to do with."

"My son's Randall Patterson. He was a captain in the first seat."

Harry couldn't believe it. "Patterson? If it's the same one, I was his radio man."

"Son of bitch, son, you two got to meet up."

"When's he coming?" asked Harry.

Wholesale slumped. "I don't know, but I'll let your friend Bobby know, soon as I hear. He'll want to meet you, that's for sure. Wouldn't that be a reunion?"

*

Members of my high-school senior class sponsor reunions every so often. I don't keep track and never attend. I'm an introvert and don't stand up well in crowds. I also fear someone will remember my mistakes and remind me. I don't know why I feel this way. If I can't remember them, they sure as hell are not going to remember me, but I'm not sure I want to take the chance. If they plan another reunion, maybe I'll stop by. If they don't, that'll be all right too.

*

Harry looked forward to seeing the captain he flew with in Korea 30 years ago. The excitement overshadowed his memory of how late he got into the war and the insignificant bombing runs they had made. During the war, Captain Patterson had flown real bombing runs, and when it was over, his radio man transferred to a secret base up north to set up high-tech equipment to spy on the Commies. Harry was only his replacement from the States.

*

With his wife sitting next to him, Randall drove his father's '41 Pontiac Torpedo along the narrow lanes of the historical cemetery,

196

until he reached the edge of the river. He parked behind a row of large tombstones facing the slow-moving dark water and reached over to his wife. Once again, passion filled the back seat of the officer's car.

*

Bobby gave his wife a kiss before it was time for her afternoon nap. He stopped at the table with Harry and introduced himself to Wholesale. When James Patterson mentioned the Enola Gay, Bobby nodded. He told Patterson the army sent him to Hiroshima with a team to assess the damage. Wholesale sat up again and leaned forward to catch every word, but after Bobby left, he remembered it made no difference at all, because he didn't get to see much of anything during the war.

*

Afternoon naps are important. If you take care of yourself, there are very few symptoms that cannot be cured by drinking water and taking an afternoon nap. When you go to bed at night, you may feel tired, but some of your day may be stirring around in our head, or some of your dinner may be stirring around in your stomach, and you might not sleep well enough to give your brain time to repair, and an un-repaired brain causes simple activities to become complex.

Naps, on the other hand, provide clear, unadulterated sleep without interruption and are more profitable because you only take them when you can no longer stand. As soon as you lie down you are out.

The completion of a nap is all the more refreshing if someone is there to ease you back into consciousness with a smile and assurance that, during your absence, they managed without you, as did the rest of the world when a million other people took a nap, correcting for time zones, at the same time.

*

Harry entered his wife's hospital room and received a big smile. She was sitting up in bed reading a magazine borrowed from her roommate. Neither one cared that much for television. He leaned over and gave her a kiss on the cheek. He thought she looked fine and wanted her to come home, but the doctors and social workers had developed a plan they knew was necessary; one they hoped would cause the least amount of family heartache and second guessing.

Harry had worked long hours for fifty-six years to support and raise his family. He knew the children would move away someday, that his memory would not hold forever, and his dreams might turn against him, but he never considered that his wife would not be there to wash it all away when he woke in the morning.

*

When I tell my wife I had a dream, and begin to fit the pieces together, the clarity and significance dissolve as quickly as she begins to smile. A dream is dredging up unrelated and randomly combined elements that had been put to rest separately in three feet of muck beneath a riverbed, behind a cemetery, where large headstones overlook the slow-moving water.

*

Randall parked the Pontiac Torpedo inside his garage. Curious about the rumored tradition his father mentioned during their cross-country trip, he opened the glove compartment to find the owner's manual. He turned to the last page left blank by the printer and added one more hashmark next to all the others.

Author's Notes

You will encounter some characters in more than one story.

The Hanging Bridge. 1947 West Virginia

While attending college in West Virginia, I was watching a poker game where one player was racking up all the chips. The other three players were not upset because it turned out they had invited him to play and show them what he knows about the game. Turned out he was a war vet and while in college, made his living playing the game. Someone asked how he protected himself driving from town to town where he didn't know anybody. "I survived the Salerno Beach invasion," he said, then reached behind his back and pulled out a revolver. "And I carry this." I don't know whatever happened to this scrappy guy, but he is my main character in *The Hanging Bridge.*

The Reporter. 1955 West Virginia

While attending college I wrote local historical pieces for the Fairmont Times which operated from 1900 to 1974 when it was taken over by a chain and renamed Times West Virginian. So, using that experience I fashioned *The Reporter* as a middle story between *The Hanging Bridge* and *Restitution*. I did meet a guy named Ike who owned a small coal mine, which I did get to visit.

Restitution. 1959 West Virginia

While visiting a family in one of West Virginia's small towns back in the hills, I was asked if I wanted to meet the Indian. "Sure," I said. "What's his name." Thy said: "His name is The

Indian. That's what everyone calls him, and he calls himself. Been around forever and nobody knows anything about him." The Indian came in the door and sat down. I have no idea where he was during our conversation. Maybe waiting for his cue. He sat without saying a word; appeared very old and looked like what I thought an Indian should look like. For *Restitution*, I created a story of his village and the motivation for the main character to set things right for his brother's false conviction and time in prison.

The Last Foxhole. 1961 West Virgina
With the exception of the last four paragraphs, everything in the story is absolutely true word for word and based on a family I lived with in a rented room while in college. To this day I cannot explain how, why, or if spirits visited this home. And yes, the husband was a World War II vet and the last survivor of his company.

Self Improvement. 2003 North Carolina.
This story is based on an event that I will never forget. I was asked to give a driving lesson to young woman married to a Marine who was somewhere else at the time. I did meet him later and he was a tough customer. I sat in the passenger seat while she constantly and dangerously hit the brakes hard whenever she saw something out of the corner of her eye. She was very timid, said very little, and I suspected was a victim of her husband's abuse. This became a revenge story that gave the young lady an opportunity to set things right. It was fun to write and became one of my favorites.

The Deer Stand. 1978 New Hampshire
This short story is basically a description of a state my wife and

I visit often, New Hampshire, with a few characters thrown in for good measure. I spent many hours selecting the scenes and words to make the story work.

The Bosses Wife. 1979 Rhode Island
Rhode Island was famous for being the headquarters of the New England Mafia until 1984 when the boss's son took over and the state police came knocking on his door. Growing up in the 50's and 60's we never gave their presence any thought. If you owned a restaurant you paid for protection, end of story. The Bosses' Wife took characters from that era and had some fun. The streets and locations are real and two of the IT characters in the story are based on those I worked with in an agency that had purchased one of my software programs.
Perfect Crime 1985 and **Guilty Party** 1986 are stories about hapless, naïve young men who lived life unaware of the dark side Two of the characters are based on friends I had in high school. and the main character is based on everyone of us who makes a mistake or two and goes through hoping no one will find out. The police detective in Guilty Party is based on a combination of my niece's husband and two detectives I met one day when they were stacking out one of my rental properties. I identified myself and asked if I have anything to worry about. They said no. Their suspect was just in the area. They gave me their card and told me to contact them if I saw anything or had a concern about a potential renter. Private investigator Anthony Duxbury is also in the story **Greater Good**.

Greater Good 1982 Rhode Island
This story is another send up to life in the Mafia. The location is

real right down to the neighborhood, elementary school, and street where we lived for six years. What do you do about a guy named who makes every assassination look like an accident and believes he's immortal? That's for Anthony to figure out. Lots of fun.

Border Crimes. 1959 Rhode Island

This is the ultimate road trip story that begins with a small newspaper in southern Rhode Island and the owner's real-life son who was well known for his questionable lifestyle. The auto garage described in the book was also real and operated just as described. It was a great place to spend Saturday mornings. While the road trip is not uneventful, you'll be glad when it's over and wonder why all the fuss until you read the last page.

Seventy-Five Cents on the Dollar. 1982 Rhode Island

This is an auto-biographical sketch that includes real events and friends I made on the tennis court. The best description of this story is printed on the back of the book.

The two supporting characters in this story Jerry and Bobby have passed away, which has saddened me greatly.

Jerry served in the Air Force and later became a machine shop foreman. Though retired, he could recount the identification number of every machine part the company produced.

Bobby served in the Navy during WW II entertaining the troops as a member of an acrobat team made up of family members. As described in the story he did go to Hiroshima to witness the destruction and did visit his wife in a nursing home every day for more than seven years. A gifted musician, he traveled around the country with the big bands playing the trombone and later the piano, which he learned to play on his own. Bob's most endearing trait, however, was his smile and his kindness that radiated into the hearts of everyone who met him. One afternoon I stopped by his house, and he told me that the day before a woman whom he had never met knocked on his door and asked to come in. Bob let her in and offered her a glass of water because she was visibly upset. Bob then asked if she was hungry. She said yes, so he made her a sandwich. During that time the woman kept looking out the window. Now during this story, I'm thinking, *'Bob you're 94 years old, 5 feet tall and weigh a hundred pounds. Why are you letting an agitated woman you don't know into your house?* Later that afternoon the police stopped by and told him the woman was running away from an abusive husband.

Bob and I were tennis partners for several years. We were known as Bob Senior and Bob Junior, and even though he's gone, I'm still Bob Junior.

Acknowledgements

During the course of writing and rewriting these stories, Patti McGovern (RI) applied her energy, enthusiasm and editing skills to keep the stories and the author focused and fused, for which I am ever grateful.

I am also thankful to Margaret Diehl (NYC) for a great job of editing out the errors found in the final version.

About the Author

Bob Sherman completed a graduate degree in education from West Virginia University and following a 33-year career in public and private school administration, designed software applications for business and public schools in Rhode Island, Massachusetts, and Connecticut and later a financial website for parents of college bound students.
The short stories in Border Crimes are based on people he has known, personal situations and historical events.
You may contact the author at:
bobsherman2@hotmail.com.

Other Books by Bob Sherman
Financial
  The Inheritance Plan   Release Date 12-1 2023
  Surviving the Cost of College
  Surviving the Cost of College Parent Handbook

Fiction
  Border Crimes and Other Stories
  The Train Station, a YA novel

Books may be ordered online through amazon by typing in the name of the book and the author's name